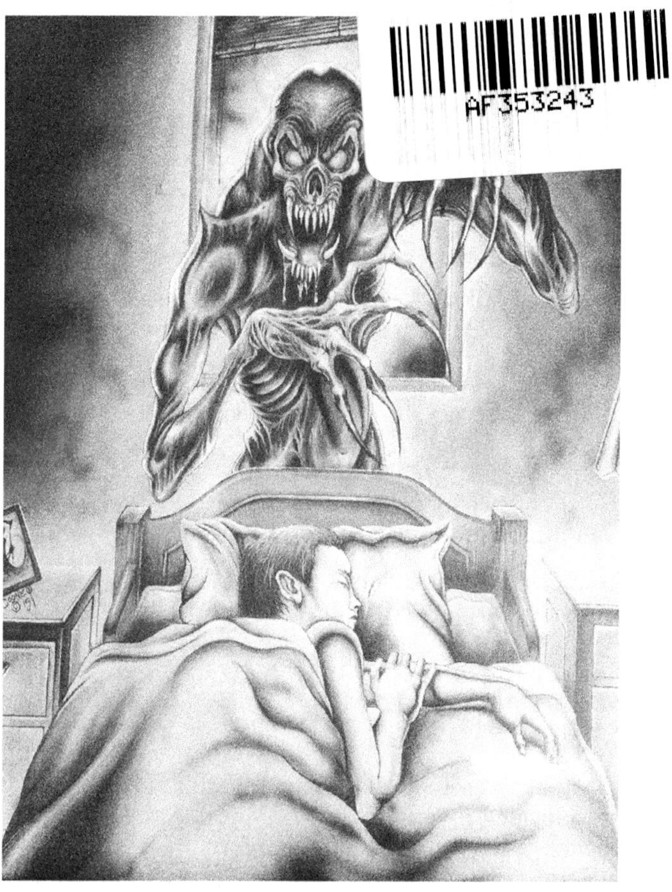

Book © James Ward Kirk Publishing
Content © Trevor Whittemore

Internet: http://www.jwkfiction.com

Twitter: @jameswardkirk

Facebook: James-Ward-Kirk-Fiction

Front Cover art by Stephen Cooney
Back Cover art and cover design by Jerry Langdon

ISBN-13: 978-94-92558-01-5
ISBN-10: 9492558017



This book is a work of fiction. Any references to historical events, real people, or real locales are used fictitiously. Any resemblance to actual events, or persons, living or dead, is coincidental.

# Table of Contents

# Chapter 1 Night Terrors

It was late September in 1996, and Ron and Tanya Walker had just purchased their first home in southern California. They lived in a small town along the outskirts of a large forest thick with trees whose hues were changing as the fall season was approaching and the temperature was dropping. It was a beautiful two-story house at the end of the street built in the 1970's, but remodeled since then. The front of the house had a two-car driveway. Just to the left, was a large archway with stone steps leading to the front door. To the right of the two-car garage was a wooden gate and to the left a door to the garage. Ron's work truck was in the garage, as his transmission needed some work. Every time he drove the truck, it would make a rattling noise as it slipped between gears. Their son Michael's room was on the right side of the house overlooking the forest, and just past the driveway was a wooden gate that led to the side of the house where the trashcans sat. A concrete path ran from the back yard to the patio. Directly above the patio was Ron and Tanya's balcony. The large back yard included pine trees and eucalyptus trees Michael loved to climb. On the left side of the house was a dirt path that led into the forest.

Inside on the right was a large staircase that led up to the master bedroom on the left. There was a computer room next to Michael's room with a window overlooking the driveway and a nursery at the end of the large upstairs hallway as Tanya was expecting a baby in about four months. They also had a family cat named Tigger who would sometimes sleep with Michael at night even though he was allergic to cats.

Ron and Tanya were starting to settle in, but Michael was having a hard time adjusting to school and life at the new home. He struggled with doing his homework and often sneaked downstairs late at night to watch TV because he couldn't sleep. With no kids in the neighborhood, he complained of being bored. Tanya even caught him sneaking girly magazines up to his room. Michael had straight brown hair and brown eyes as well, and he wore glasses. He was as smart as he was brave, but he had a hard time making friends. One day as he played in his room, the door opened.

"Hey son, can I talk to you for a minute?" his dad asked. Michael followed Ron downstairs to the TV room. Ron was in his early forties and in great shape. He had dark brown hair and eyes and spent his weekdays building houses.

Ron sat Michael down on his black leather sofa to try to find the underlying cause of things.

"Hey, bud. How's things been going?" he asked Michael.

He shrugged his shoulders.

"Come on. What's going on?"

"Phillip picks on me."

"What's he do?"

"He calls me names and shoots spit wads at me." Michael grabbed a pillow from the couch.

"And what do you do?"

Michael paused for a moment hunching over the pillow as he looked down at his feet. "I told the teacher, but at lunch he punched me in the stomach and stole my chocolate milk."

"Well, that is not acceptable and you have a right to defend yourself if he does it again."

"What do you mean?"

"Here, come with me." Michael started to follow his dad through the house. They stopped halfway. "You want to know something, son?"

"Sure," said Michael giving his full attention to his dad.

"You know I grew up in New York. I was a pretty good fighter at one time."

"Wow, really?" asked Michael.

"Yeah, really. They used to call me One, Two, Ronny Walker because after the second punch my opponent would be out for the count."

"That's awesome, Dad."

"Your mom would come to all my fights to cheer me on when we first started dating."

"Cool. How come you don't fight anymore?"

"Well I would have gone pro, but I hurt my back trying to move a heavy boulder by myself at work. I went to the doctor and he took an x-ray and told me that I had slipped a disc. Later I needed back surgery."

"So that's where you got that scar on your back."

"It sure is. It ended my career as a fighter. But you know, I'm also grateful because your mom never left my side during my recovery. Less than a year later we were married."

"That story is true, sweetie," said Tanya, as she overheard the whole thing. She was preparing dinner. Ron gave her a wink.

Tanya was a beautiful woman with light straight brown hair and beautiful brown eyes. She was very attractive and had a nice figure that she kept from doing yoga with her best friend Crystal. Tanya was in charge of paying the bills, getting the groceries, cooking, as well as being a stay at home mom.

Michael followed him out to the patio directly under his balcony where Ron had hung a large black Everlast punching bag. "Now put up your hands and ball them into a fist.

Michael clenched his fists.

"Don't hold onto your thumbs. If you hit someone like that, you could break them. Watch me." Ron showed him the proper way to make a fist then took a swing at the bag, making it sway.

"Wow," said Michael. "You hit hard."

"Now it's your turn, bud." Michael imitated his dad's punch, making the bag swing a little.

"Wow, what a punch. I am going to have to start calling you Mike Tyson." Michael laughed and his dad squeezed against his stomach as he rubbed his head.

"Next time that kid messes with you that punch will make him think twice. Don't tell your mom. I don't want her to worry any more than she already does."

"I won't, Dad. I promise."

"That a boy. Now let's eat."

"Dad."

"Yeah?"

"There's something else."

"What's up?"

"I've been having this really scary dream, but I'm not sure if it's really a dream because sometimes I'm awake when I see it."

"Is it the one you told me about with the kid missing his eyes?"

"No. It's worse than that."

"Worse than that? Tell me about it."

"There's this black monster, and he lives in the forest, and he watches me through my window when I'm in bed."

"What does this monster look like?"

"He has red eyes. But they're not normal eyes. And he has these really long, sharp, pointy, teeth and long fingers with sharp black claws at the end of them, and he eats kids."

"Well, that does sound pretty scary, but you know what? It's just a dream."

"But I'm awake sometimes when I see it."

"You know there's no such thing as monsters, right?"

"Yeah, I guess so, but when I wake up it feels so real. Last night he was standing right over me."

"Next time you have this dream, I want you to turn on the light, and you'll see that it's nothing. When I was little, I used to think a giant alligator was going to crawl up from the sewer by my house and eat me!"

"Really?" said Michael. "What did you do?"

"I waited for him outside with a BB gun one night."

"Did you get him?"

Ron chuckled. "No. My dad woke me up and tanned my hide. The alligator turned out to be nothing more than my overactive imagination. I love you bud, and I won't let anything happen to you. Now how about we enjoy some of that lasagna your mom has worked so hard on?"

After Michael finished his dinner, he helped his dad with the dishes and went to the living room to watch some TV before bed.

"No horror movies," said Ron.

Ron talked with Tanya in the kitchen while Michael watched TV. He told her about Michael's dreams and about the monster. He saw the uneasiness in her face.

"Don't worry," he said. "I talked to him, and he's all right."

"He's been struggling at home and at school and now this. Don't you think it's time we did something?"

"Let's give him a chance. He's tougher than he looks. Believe me baby! He has a punch that could knock me down."

Tanya's face grew red. She clenched her jaw. "So teaching our kid how to fight is going to solve everything?"

"No, but at least that bully will think twice before picking on him again."

Tanya smiled awkwardly.

"You're right babe. I'm sorry I got upset. It just pains me to see him struggle." She teared up as she held him.

"It's all right, baby. He'll be just fine. You'll see." He stroked her long brown hair and kissed her cheek.

"I'm going to work on my truck for a bit"

"You do that, handsome." She finished up in the kitchen and went to the TV room to check on Michael.

"What are you watching, sweetie?"

"Goosebumps!"

She put her hands on her hips. "Michael Anthony Walker, your dad told you no horror movies."

"It's for kids though."

"Not at night."

"But that's the only time it's on. Please Mom."

She picked up the remote and turned off the TV. "No means no, mister." Ron came back inside and walked into the TV room.

"Everything ok?" he asked.

"He's watching horror movies."

"I said no horror. That stuff isn't good for your mind, especially before you go to sleep. Come on. It's bed time."

"Just ten more minutes. Please ,Dad?"

"No. Now, Michael."

Michael trudged up the stairs, his head hung in disappointment. Ron followed him and tucked him. He kissed his head and turned off the light.

"No!" Michael yelled. Ron turned the light back on.

"What's wrong?" he asked.

"He can get me in the dark. Please leave the light on. Please, Dad."

"Okay," Ron said and turned the light back on. "It's not good to sleep with the light on, though."

"But it comes from the dark."

"Michael, there are no such things as monsters."

"Please Dad. Leave it on."

"Ok, but I want you to think about getting a nightlight soon."

"Ok."

"I'm just down the hall you don't have to worry about a thing."

"Thanks Dad."

"You know I love you, right?"

"Yeah, I love you too, Dad."

"Before I forget, what would you like for your birthday?"

"A BMX bike."

"If you start doing better in school and behaving at home, then you might just get one."

"I will, Dad."

They said goodnight, and Ron headed to his bedroom for a hot shower. When he hopped into bed, Tanya was lying in bed watching TV. "This monster business is becoming a real problem."

"What did he say now?"

"He won't sleep without the light. He's terrified of this thing he's been dreaming about. I can hear it in his voice."

"Maybe we should take him to see someone to talk about it."

Ron bolted up. "What? So they can put him on meds. I don't think so."

"I didn't say that, babe. I just think it will be good for someone who specializes in these things to talk to him so we can understand it better."

"I don't want our kid walking around like a zombie, doped out of his mind. I mean he's already losing sleep. Last week he told me he saw a dead kid with no eyes for fuck sake. What kid dreams of shit like that? He's only eight years old for Christ's sake."

"Shit. That is scary."

"Tell me about it." He looked deep into Tanya's eyes. "Don't you worry, babe. I won't let anything happen to our Michael." He kissed her goodnight and rolled over.

Thoughts of the monster Ron had described filled Tanya's head and kept her awake. She went to the bathroom for some Valium. As she closed the medicine cabinet, a boy with empty, bleeding eye sockets stared back at her in the mirror. She screamed and dropped her glass of water in the sink. Ron dashed in.

"Are you ok? What is it? What happened?" he asked.

"A big spider crawled up through the drain. It scared me half to death." Tanya's heart raced as terror gripped it.

"You poor thing," Ron said as he leaned over and kissed her head. "Go back to bed. I'll take care of the mess." Tanya headed to bed and he put the shards of glass in the wastebasket. A large piece of glass cut deep into his finger. "Ah shit," he whispered and pulled it out. His finger gushed. He cleaned it, wrapped it in gauze, and went back to bed.

*****

Michael lay awake in his bed listening to a scratching noise outside his door and picturing the monster from his dreams. His heartbeat increased, but he took a deep breath and said, "It's nothing to be afraid of. It isn't real. I will punch it in the face if it is." He got up to investigate and discovered Tigger on the other side of the door. He let out a deep breath.

"Don't scare me like that boy," said Michael as he stroked Tigger's long fur. He put him in bed with him and petted him until he fell asleep.

He woke from another nightmare about 3 am. He put on his glasses and gazed out his bedroom window. Wind rustled the leaves of the forest, but there was no monster. It was only another bad dream.

"Hey boy," he said to Tigger.

"I know you'll keep me safe."

As he headed back to bed, a voice whispered from under his sheet where Tigger was lying,

"Michael, it isn't safe." He yanked back the sheet and instead of Tigger, the severed head of a boy looked up at him.

"Leave this place," it said.

Michael screamed and threw the covers back over the head. He ran as fast as he could to his parents' room. He screamed and cried as he pounded his fists against their door. Ron opened the door and Michael grabbed his legs, Tanya stood behind him, a little sluggish from the Valium.

"What is it?" Ron asked him as he knelt down, putting his hands on his cheeks.

Michael didn't speak but wrapped his arms around his dad's neck and held him tightly.

What is it sweetie?" said Tanya as she got down on her knees and put her hand on his shoulder.

Ron rubbed Michael's head.

"Hey it's okay, slugger. I'm here. Tell me what's wrong."

"Ron, he is white as a sheet and soaking wet."

Michael pointed toward his bedroom, his mouth open, and terror in his eyes.

"What did you see, son?" asked Ron.

"A boy's head. In my bed."

"It was just a bad dream, slugger."

"No, Dad. It was real."

The hairs on the back of Ron's neck tingled. He grabbed Michael's hand and walked with him toward his bedroom. Michael pulled away and ran back to his parents' room. He grabbed tightly onto Tanya's waist. She knelt down and squeezed him tight. "Everything is okay, honey. It was just a bad dream," she told him.

Ron's heart raced as he stood in Michael's room. He peeled back the covers picturing the severed head of a child in his mind. But he was much relieved to find Tigger fast asleep. He took a deep breath and headed back to his room. He grabbed Michael's hand gently.

"There's nothing to be scared of. Come with me. I'll show you."

Michael hesitated." Its okay, sweetie, go with your dad. You'll see. There's nothing to worry about," said Tanya. Ron showed him Tigger lying where the boy's head had been minutes ago.

"See. I told you there was nothing to be afraid of. It's just Tigger."

"But a head was right there. He called my name and told me to leave this place. I swear. It's coming for me!"

"Settle down," Ron said. "Nothing is coming after you. If there were, I'd bust his ass in two. You have nothing to worry about."

That head Michael had seen was 100% real and so was the voice. He begged his dad to let him sleep in bed with him and his mom.

"Just for tonight." Michael nodded and Ron carried him to bed. He lay him down next to his mom and got into bed. "I love you, Michael."

"I love you too, Dad."

# Chapter 2 Bullied

The next morning Tanya and Ron agreed it was time to take Michael to see a therapist. Tanya had made Michael his favorite scrambled eggs. He shoveled them into his mouth and drank his orange juice. Tanya enjoyed cooking for Michael as much as he enjoyed eating what she cooked for him.

"How was your breakfast?"

"Good. Thanks Mom." Tanya put her hand on Michael's head.

"Honey, today you and I are going to see someone who can help you with these dreams you've been having," she told him.

"Who?"

"His name is Dr. Donahue, and I think he could help."

"I don't want to go."

"Why honey? He might be able to help them go away. How about we at least give it a try."

"Ok. If you think it will help.

"I think it will. Come here and give your mom a hug."

He did, and she handed him his lunch.

"Thanks, Mom," he said as he grabbed his backpack from a hook.

"You're welcome, honey. Have a good day in school!"

"I will," he said and put his lunch into his backpack and headed out the door for the bus stop.

*****

Something hit Michael in the head when he was writing down his homework assignment in Math class.

"Phillip Gibbons, go to the office this minute," Mrs. Stone said. As Phillip stormed out of the classroom he gave Michael the evil eye and Michael gave him a dirty look right back. When Michael looked down on the floor, he saw the large pink, rubber eraser that Phillip had just thrown at him. Within a few minutes, Mrs. Stone received a phone call from the office. "Michael, come here for a minute, dear," she said. "Your mother just called, and you have a doctor's appointment today at 3:00. She will be picking you up from school, so wait for her outside."

Minutes later the lunch bell rang, and all of the children rushed out the door. Michael ate his lunch in the classroom. Mrs. Stone reassured him that the next time Phillip did something like that she would have him suspended. "You're a good kid, Michael," she said. She smiled and patted his head, and he went outside to play.

As Michael walked across the blacktop, something harder and larger hit him in the back of the head, knocking his glasses to the ground. When he turned, the blurry figure behind him said, " You little bastard. You got me in trouble." Phillip stood with a basketball in his hands. Phillip strutted toward him. Michael took a swing at him and connected with Phillip's nose. It gushed blood as he fell to the ground screaming and crying. Michael felt satisfaction and relief as if the weight of the world had been lifted from his shoulders as he was now in control. A proctor quickly intervened, grabbing both boys by their shirts. He dropped Phillip at the nurse's office on his way to taking Michael to Principal O'Riley's office.

"This young man just punched Phillip Gibbons in the face," he told the principal.

"I see the blood on your hand. Sit." Michael sat. "Why an earth would you punch Phillip in the face?" Michael explained to him that Phillip had picked on him every day since he had been going to Forest Pines Elementary School. "What kind of things does he do?"

Michael told him Philip called him a geek and threw things at him. "And at lunch he takes my chocolate milk and punches me in the stomach. Today he threw a basketball at my head."

"You know it's not ok to hurt people, even if they do have it coming."

"Yes, Principal O'Riley."

The principal called the nurse's office and had her bring Phillip to him. Blood covered Phillip's shirt. He held an ice pack over his very swollen nose.

"Take a seat, please," Principal O'Riley said and motioned to a chair next to Michael. Phillip hesitated for a moment, but sat down, as he did not want to upset the principal. Michael and Phillip exchanged glances. "You know, I have heard of you bullying kids before but what you have done to Michael is downright cruel."

"But he punched me in the face!" Phillip said.

"And you know darned well why, don't you?" asked Principal O'Riley.

"Because I am mean to him," Phillip muttered.

"Speak up. I can't hear you."

"Because I'm mean to him."

"Well what the heck for?" asked Principal O'Riley. "He didn't bully you now did he?"

"No," said Phillip.

"He didn't throw a basketball at your head and call you a geek did he?"

"No."

"He didn't take your chocolate milk or punch you in the stomach did he?"

"No he didn't," said Phillip.

"I want you to apologize to him for all the nasty things you have done to him."

"I'm sorry for being a bully," Phillip said to Michael.

"It's ok. I'm sorry I hit you," said Michael.

"It's ok," said Phillip.

The principal told them to shake hands. "If either of you does this kind of thing again, you'll both be suspended from school. Violence is not the answer." He told Michael to wash his hands and dismissed them both.

As they left, Phillip asked Michael if he wanted to hang out at his house with him after school the next day.

"Sure," said Michael. "That would be fun." Michael went to the boys' room and washed his hands.

As he pushed the school doors open at the end of the day, he saw his mom waving at him from her station wagon. He waved back and got into the car

"How was your day, sweetie?"

"It was good! Can I go over to Phillip's house after school tomorrow?"

"I thought you didn't like that kid."

"Well he was nice to me today."

"Really I thought you two were enemies."

"Not anymore."

"Well that is good to hear." She looked at Michael and noticed blood on his sleeve. She pulled over the car.

"What the hell happened?"

"I'm sorry, Mom. I didn't want to upset you."

"What do you mean upset me? Is that someone else's blood?"

Michael looked down at his feet.

"Tell me the truth, Michael!"

"It's Phillip's. I punched him in the nose because he threw something at my head, and then at recess he threw a basketball at my head, and I just punched him after that."

"Did you get into trouble?"

"No. He got into more trouble than I did and then he asked me if I wanted to come over to his house and play tomorrow."

"I guess he learned his lesson."

"I guess so."

"I don't want you to think hitting other kids is okay. I don't condone violence."

"I know. I'm not a bully though."

"I know you were defending yourself, and I'm glad you two can become friends now."

"Yeah, I am too," he said with a smile.

# Chapter 3 Dr. Donahue

At the doctor's office, she walked him in and the receptionist handed her a clipboard with papers to fill out. Not long after, a heavyset man with glasses and a white beard opened the door and called Michael and his mom back. He introduced himself as Dr. Donahue.

"It's nice to meet you," said Tanya.

"Likewise," he said. "And you must be Michael."

"Yes sir." Michael shook Dr. Donahue's hand.

"Please. This way," he said and led Michael and Tanya into his office before shutting the door. "So how old are you, Michael?"

"I'm eight."

"So that would put you in what, second grade?"

"No, I just started third."

"He will be turning nine in a week," Tanya added.

"Well then a happy early birthday to you," said Dr. Donahue.

"Thanks," said Michael with a smile.

"So then, Michael, how are things going at school for you?" Dr. Donahue asked.

"Well there was this bully named Phillip, but we became friends today, and I'm going to his house after school tomorrow to play."

"We will see," said Tanya.

"Well that is good you two became friends. How did that happen?"

Michael told him the whole story about how Phillip had treated him. "So today I got so angry when he threw a basketball at my head that I punched him in the nose, and now we're friends," he said.

"I'm sorry to hear that but also happy to hear you to are friends. Fighting isn't always the answer, you know."

"Yeah, I know."

"Good. How are things at home?"

"Fine, except for these bad dreams I've been having.

"What kind of bad dreams?" Dr. Donahue asked.

"I'd rather not say."

Dr. Donahue asked Tanya to wait outside for a few minutes.

"Okay Michael. Tell me about your dream."

"Well there's this scary monster, and it comes for me at night."

"You mean when you fall asleep?"

"Well, sometimes, but not last night."

"What do you mean by that?"

"I woke up after I had a bad dream about the monster watching me. I had my cat with me, but when I heard my name, I pulled back the sheet and . . . "

Michael trembled as he remembered what had happened.

"It's ok, Michael. You can tell me. You don't have to be frightened in here. I promise."

"When I pulled back the sheet, Tigger was gone, and there was a boy's head there instead, and it told me to leave my house!"

"Did the head say anything else?"

"I ran to my mom and dad's room and got my dad."

"And what happened?"

"He found my cat Tigger in my bed."

"Michael, did you know that there is a name for what you experienced?"

"It was not a bad dream. I was awake when I saw."

"No, you are right. It was not a dream. It was a night terror."

"What is a night terror?"

"A night terror is something many children just like yourself experience. Even the scariest things can seem real, but they're not. Do you understand what I mean?"

"Not really."

"Well, your cat Tigger, for instance, looked like a child's head but then it actually wasn't. They're called hallucinations. Many kids with night terrors see things like monsters that are not real. What if I told you I have a special pill that could make these monsters go away?"

"I would take it," said Michael.

"Good answer. Now how about you go and get your mom." He asked her to take a seat when she entered the room. "How is Michael doing in school?"

"He's struggling a bit in Math and Social Studies. It's hard for him to sit still in class sometimes."

"And how is he at home?"

"He's good, but he puts up a struggle when asked to do homework and chores sometimes. His nightmares are the biggest problem."

"I believe Michael suffers from pavor Nocturnus."

"Pa what?" said Tanya.

"Pavor Nocturnus—it means night terrors. It's a condition where the child appears awake, but they are actually asleep. They can have pretty vivid hallucinations."

"That's scary. Is there anything we can do to stop them?"

"Yes, there is a pill called Tofranil that works quite well for this kind of thing, and it should also help Michael keep his focus at school."

"It won't make him dopey or anything, will it?" she asked.

"Well he should take them at night, and he shouldn't have a problem sleeping through the night while he is on it. It has also been proven to help children who have been struggling with their schoolwork."

"I guess we can try it," she said.

"Good. I'll give you some samples I have here, and if they do the trick, I'll write you a prescription. I want him taking one pill a night before bedtime. "

"Wonderful. Thank you," said Tanya.

"You're welcome, and if these night terrors persist, I want you to bring him back to see me immediately."

That night Michael took one after dinner. His dad put him to bed not long after.

"How did it go with the therapist?" he asked Tanya.

She explained to him that Michael had been suffering from night terrors, and that Dr. Donahue gave him a pill that would help with his night terrors and help him focus at school.

"As long as it doesn't make him a zombie; if it does, then I don't want him taking it."

# Chapter 4 It's Real

Later that night Michael found himself standing in the hallway of his house, but older carpet lined the floor. He opened the door to his parents' room, and in the bed lay a large man in a wife beater with empty bottles of alcohol everywhere. The laughter of kids came from the two rooms at the very end of the hallway. When he reached the door to one of them, he opened it and saw four boys. Three of them were jumping up and down on a large bed with a big black sheet over it.

"Why aren't you bouncing with us, Mike Collins? Afraid of falling?" asked one of the boys.

"No, I don't feel like it," a boy replied. He grasped a medal he was wearing around his neck. "You guys should stop," he said.

"Come on, Mike. This is fun. You should join us", said one of the boys.

The light in the room flickered, and Mike told them to get off the bed, but before they could, the black monster Michael had seen in his dreams rose from the middle of the black sheet. It grabbed one of the kids by his neck with its long sharp black clawed hand. The light in the room exploded, then screams, followed by tearing, crunching, and cracking sounds. Mike ran like crazy down the hall, and Michael followed him into a closet. He pulled the chain on a hanging light bulb to turn it on. Mike held his breath so that the monster would not hear him. To his right was a large black trench coat on a hanger. The creature's arm reached out of it and grabbed Mike by the neck. He grabbed the monster's arm and screamed as he tried to pull it off, but its grip was too tight to break free. Mike's screams faded into Tigger meowing rather strangely.

Michael woke, gasping for air. His alarm clock read 3:00 am. Tigger continued to meow unnaturally and as Michael followed Tigger's gaze, it was pitch black but he saw something move in the darkness of the shelf above his closet. Tigger hissed, and Michael quickly turned on the light and fixed his gaze toward the movement. There was nothing there. His heart raced as he picked up Tigger and stood on his bed to look deeper into the dark shadowed corner of his shelf above his closet. He saw nothing. Tigger peered over Michael's left shoulder. A black arm reached straight up from Michael's black dresser, and with its long clawed finger, it flicked the light bulb in the lamp, shattering it to pieces. Tigger dug his claws deep into Michael's skin, leaped off Michael, and ran out of the room.

Michael grabbed his glasses off the floor and quickly turned as his lamp fell to the carpet. Out of his dresser emerged something dark, something sinister, and something not of this world. It was terrifying. It had long sharp translucent fangs, and crimson red eyes. At the end of its long arms were black claws that almost appeared as part of its fingers. The monster was black with a concave nose like a skeleton's, and it stunk of death and rot. Michael froze in fear and peed himself out of sheer terror. As it reached for him, he jumped from his bed and into the hallway, slamming the door shut behind him. He ran down the long hallway, and the lights flickered off and on. He couldn't get to his parents' room fast enough. His bedroom door opened as he reached his parents' door, and the creature broke the hallway light with its hand. Michael tried to open his parents' door but it was locked. He pounded on it while screaming at the top of his lungs. As he looked over his shoulder, the dark creature came closer and closer. It let out a sinister hissing growl, and Michael screamed, "Help Dad. It's coming for me. Please help," he cried as loud as he could.

*****

Ron grabbed a baseball bat from his closet and opened the door. He grabbed Michael's hand. He was sweating and crying.

"What's the matter, sweetie?" Tanya picked him up.

"The monster is after me," he said. Michael's eyes and mouth were open wide, and he was huffing and puffing after just seeing the same monster from his nightmares come to life before his eyes. Tanya immediately knew something was wrong. She saw that he had wet himself.

Ron noticed the dark hallway. "What's the matter, slugger?" he asked.

"It's in my room. It came out of the top of my dresser."

"I told you we shouldn't have fucking put him on any medication," Ron said to Tanya.

"Will you just look? Our son just wet himself for Christ's sake?" she replied. Thoughts of the child she had seen in the mirror the night before filled her mind.

"Okay, but I am going to have words with this Dr. Donahue."

Ron put on his slippers and stepped carefully as he approached Michael's room with the baseball bat in hand, broken glass from the light bulb crunching under his feet. *How in the hell did this happen*, he thought as he pulled open the door to Michael's room. It was completely dark inside, and the smell of rotten meat was strong from within. As he entered, he stepped on one of Michael's action figures.

"Son of a bitch," he yelled.

"Are you okay in there?" asked Tanya.

"Yeah, yeah, I'm fine." He ran into the bathroom door as he crossed the hallway. "Fucking door." He opened the bathroom door and turned the light on so that he could see inside Michael's room. When he went back into Michael's room, he noticed the lamp on the black dresser had fallen to the floor. The light bulb must have shattered. He checked inside the closet and saw nothing, but when he closed the mirrored doors, he saw the reflection of something very tall in the corner of the room. He thought it might just be a shadow until he saw a pair of red eyes. He swung the baseball bat at the figure and knocked a large hole in the wall. There was nothing there.

"What the hell was that, Ron? Are you okay?"

Tanya rushed into the hallway when he didn't answer.

"Ouch," Tanya's voice came from the hall. Ron rushed into the hall where she was leaning against the wall holding her foot.

"Are you okay, babe? What happened?"

"I just stepped on some glass."

"Are you bleeding?"

"No luckily I am not, but please clean up that glass, Ron. I don't have my slippers on." Michael called for her. "One minute, Michael." She looked at Ron. "What is it?"

"I swear I just saw someone in Michael's mirror."

"Tell me you're kidding," she said.

"I wish I were."

"What the hell happened?"

"I thought I saw someone in the mirror, standing right over there. I took a swing at him but it was nothing. Maybe it's just too much excitement for one night, but right now I need you to get me my Maglite."

Tanya carefully walked back to her room, put on her slippers, and grabbed Ron's Maglite from her closet. He turned it on and immediately noticed the bronze lamp on the floor and that the bulb was busted inside of it. Shards of glass were on Michael's dresser and scattered about the room. He cleaned up all the glass and checked under Michael's bed, on his shelf, and in the closet. He found nothing.

"I'm going to check the rest of the house just to be safe," he said.

"Be careful," said Tanya.

"I will." Michael called for his mom. "Stay with Michael."

He walked through the rest of the house, turning on every light as he went. He searched under every bed and inside every closet, behind every curtain, but nothing turned up. He looked in the computer room and out the window but saw nothing. He went to the nursery and searched, but there was no one hiding in there. He cleaned up the broken glass in the hallway and returned to the bedroom.

"Is everything all right?" Tanya said.

"Yeah, nobody's here."

"So what did you think you saw?"

"It must have been a shadow in the mirror."

"No. It was the monster. It's real. I saw it," Michael insisted.

"No it wasn't, Michael. It was nothing at all."

"That's not true. It's after me," he said.

Ron turned to look at Tanya. "We need to do something about this. I don't want him taking this medication ever again. I can't deal with this every fucking night." He locked the bedroom door and lay down next to Michael as he cried in their bed. Ron rubbed his head. "It's okay, slugger. No one is after you. I'm here, bud."

Michael was asleep in minutes.

"Ron, I saw something the other night as well," Tanya said.

"What did you see?"

"I think I saw the same kid Michael has been seeing, the one with no eyes."

"Why in the hell did–"

"Shhh, quiet, he's sleeping."

"Why the hell didn't you tell me this before?" he whispered.

"Because at first I wasn't sure myself, and I didn't want to say anything in front of Michael. But what if this place really is really haunted?"

"Don't say that. Well maybe there is a reason we got it so cheap. That's the last fucking thing I need on my mind right now."

"Maybe we can look into it."

"You can look into it if you're that worried."

"Thanks a lot," she said and turned onto her side.

"Don't mention it."

*Well if you won't listen to me, I know Crystal will*, she thought.

The next morning Ron kissed Michael on the head before he left. Tanya was up soon after, and she woke Michael for school. He still looked a bit shook up.

"You okay?" she asked him.

"I want to get the fuck out of this place," he said.

"Michael Anthony Walker, don't you swear like that."

"But something bad is after me. It's real. I saw it. Where is Dad?"

"He's at work, sweetie."

"He saw the black monster in my room, didn't he?"

"There is no black monster, Michael. You had another night terror."

"I did not. It came for me and almost got me last night. Please Mom; don't make me stay in this house."

"I'm keeping you home from school today. We're going to see Dr. Donahue and get to the bottom of this."

"No, I have got to go to school. I told Phillip I would come over after. Please Mom."

"Okay, but I'm making you another appointment to see the doctor."

"Fine," he said. "Can you get my clothes for me? Please Mom?" he asked as he crossed his hands behind his back.

"No, but I can come with you to get them if you would like."

"Okay, but you go first."

As she entered Michael's room, she noticed a rancid smell, like when she lived in New York and a rat died in her wall. She peered through the large hole Ron had made with the bat and smelled inside it. It wasn't coming from the hole. It was coming from the room.

"It's the monster. He smells bad," Michael said.

Tanya picked the lamp up off the floor. As she reached to put it back on the black dresser, Michael stopped her. "Don't Mom."

"Why?"

"That's where the stinky black monster came from."

Tanya stared at the dresser then leaned down and smelled it. Sure enough, that was where the smell was coming from. A slimy black residue covered the top of his dresser. "What on earth is this stuff?" she asked.

"It's monster slime. Don't touch it," he said as he backed up against the wall.

She asked Michael if he had seen Tigger anywhere outside or inside the house.

"The monster scared him away."

Tanya's face reddened. She grabbed his shoulder. "Stop lying to me."

Michael screamed. "Ouch!"

"I didn't grab you that hard!"

"Tigger scratched me," said Michael as he lifted his shirt to show his mom the claw marks.

"That's not like Tigger to do that."

"He saw the monster before I did and clawed me."

Things were getting weirder by the moment.

"Come with me." She took Michael to her bathroom, cleaned, and dressed his wound. "You know I love you."

"Yeah, I know."

"And you can tell me anything. You don't have to lie to me."

"I know, Mom. I'm not lying to you. I swear to you I'm not."

"Okay honey. Are you sure it wasn't a man you saw who might have come through your window."

"No, it was a black monster with long sharp teeth and red eyes. Mom, I'm scared. I don't want him to get me." He squeezed her legs in his arms.

*****

"Be on standby in case I need to come get you from school," Tanya said as he headed for the door.

"What about Phillip?"

"We will see. Give me a hug." She reached out her arms, but he pulled away and dashed out the door.

Although it made sense that Tigger knocked the lamp over in Michael's room, she was puzzled as to how the hallway light got broken and where that stinky black slimy stuff came from, unless of course Michael did it. She cleaned up all of the glass and slime and jumped in the shower.

As she slipped on some jeans and a black tunic, thoughts of the monster raced through her head. That terrible smell in his room was unlike anything she had ever smelled before. Something was not right. Where is Tigger? She searched the house but couldn't find him anywhere. Before she knew it, a few hours had passed and she decided to call Dr. Donahue. She told him Michael had a bad reaction to the Tofranil.

"What kind of reaction?" he asked.

"I have never seen anyone so scared in my entire life," she said. "He swears to me he saw a monster last night and you know- oh never mind." She wanted to tell him about everything else but stopped herself, as she did not want him trying to analyze her too.

"What?"

"I'm just worried the pill made him this way."

"Well one of the more rare side effects is vivid hallucinations. I don't want him taking it again."

"Oh, he won't be."

"I would like to see Michael again soon so we can discuss a more feasible plan of action."

"No more meds."

"I don't want to put him on anything more. I want to take a different approach to this."

"What kind of approach?"

"Hypnosis."

"Is it dangerous?"

"Harmless, I promise you."

"I am going to have to talk it over with Ron first."

"That is fine when can you bring him in next?"

"How about on Monday at 3pm, will that work?"

"Monday will be fine. I will see the both of you on Monday."

"See you then." Tanya hung up the phone, picked it right back up, and called Crystal who quickly answered.

"Hello Crystal. How are you?"

"How have you been?" asked Crystal

"Well things have been better."

"What's wrong, honey?"

Tanya cried. "It's Michael."

"What happened?"

"He's been having night terrors."

"What do you mean?"

"I am exhausted. The past few nights he's been waking up really late, convinced he saw a monster in his room."

"Wow. I am sorry to hear that. He is just having bad dreams."

"I'm not so sure."

"Aww, sweetie, how about you come over here, and I'll make us some sandwiches and cheesecake."

"That sounds good. What time?" Tanya sniffed and wiped tears from her eyes.

"Now is fine with me."

"Give me fifteen, and I will be over."

She decided to look at Michael's room one last time before leaving. When she got upstairs, she noticed she had forgotten to put new light bulbs in the hallway fixture and the lamp in Michael's room so she grabbed two new light bulbs and replaced the broken ones in the hallway and in Michael's room. That terrible smell lingered in Michael's room, and she couldn't help but wonder what could have made such a stink. She sprayed Lysol in his room then grabbed her purse and keys and left for Crystal's house.

# Chapter 5 Best Friends

When she arrived at Crystal's house, she rang her doorbell. Crystal answered wearing a flowered summer dress. She hugged Tanya and invited her in. "I made us some sandwiches. Are you hungry?

"Starving," said Tanya as she followed Crystal into the kitchen and took a seat at the kitchen table. "This looks good. What is it?" she asked as Crystal placed a large sub sandwich in front of her and a glass of lemonade.

"It's buffalo mozzarella caprese with prosciutto and Genoa salami on a French roll, with fresh tomato and basil from my garden!"

Tanya took a bite. "This is the best sandwich I've ever tasted," she said after swallowing.

"Thanks, hon."

"It's been a while. How have things been with you, anyone new in your life?" asked Tanya.

"Not since Tony was locked up"

"You need to find yourself a good man, Crystal. You deserve it."

"I will when the time's right."

"I am sure you will. You are one of the most beautiful women I have ever seen."

"Aww thank you, sweetie, you're pretty hot yourself. So how are you and Ron doing?"

"We are long overdue for a date night," said Tanya, her mouth half full of food.

"Let me know if you need me to watch Michael."

"Thank you. I sure will." Tanya wiped her face.

"You said over the phone you were having problems with Michael."

Tears came to her eyes. Crystal hugged her. "It's ok, honey." She handed Tanya a tissue.

"Thanks," she replied, taking the tissue. "It has just been crazy these past two nights."

"What happened?"

"Michael started having bad dreams. He was waking up late, saying he saw some kid's head in his bed. I told Ron I thought we should take him to see someone about it. It's affecting all of us. He agreed but he didn't want him on medication. I found him a therapist and he gave me a pill called Tofranil. He said it would help Michael sleep without having night terrors. That didn't work, and Ron got angry at me."

"I am sorry," said Crystal, handing Tanya another Kleenex. Tanya wiped her eyes and nose. "You said on the phone something about a monster." Tanya took a drink of her lemonade.

"Yes. Michael has been dreaming of some kind of black monster. Last night it scared him so bad he nearly broke down our door screaming and crying. It scared me half to death. The scariest thing is when Ron went to look in Michael's room. He saw something in the mirror. He swung a bat at it and knocked a big hole in the wall."

"No way. What was it?"

"Ron searched the entire house and didn't find anything. Last night I stepped on some glass in the hallway. The hall light bulb was broken in pieces on the floor. And the light bulb in Michael's room was broken this morning."

"That is strange."

"I thought Tigger may have knocked the lamp off his dresser, but this terrible smell was coming from where the lamp was. Michael said the monster came out of the top of the dresser." Tanya's lemonade sloshed in its glass.

"That is scary, are you okay? You look a little shaky."

"I don't think so."

"Take some breaths with me, girl," said Crystal.

Tanya inhaled in through her nose and out through her mouth.

"Are you okay now?" asked Crystal.

"Yes I am. Thanks."

"Okay, go on."

"I noticed claw marks on Michael. He said the cat scratched him when it saw the monster. I haven't seen Tigger since yesterday. I looked everywhere for that cat."

"I am so sorry, honey," said Crystal. Tanya told her about the boy in the medicine cabinet mirror who had no eyes. "That is creepy. Do you think the place is haunted?"

"I asked Ron that same question last night. He's too busy to care."

"Well I have internet. We might be able to find something out about the place."

They looked up Tanya's address and at the top of the list of results was a link to a story titled "Child Murderer Found Guilty". Tanya's heart raced as Crystal clicked on the link. It took them to a newspaper article stating that on October 6th of 1976 Robert Collins murdered three boys. A picture showed a police officer putting Robert into a squad car. The article said it was a triple homicide and that the mutilated bodies of Andrew Miller, Nathan Johnson, and Brandon Burkhart were found in the room above the garage.

"Oh, my god. That happened in my computer room"

According to the article, authorities later found Robert's son Michael Collins hiding in a tree behind his house in a state of shock.

Tanya couldn't believe what she was reading. She looked at the picture of the three murdered boys and her heart nearly stopped. Nathan Johnson was the boy she had seen in the mirror, the child who was missing his eyes.

"That's him," she exclaimed.

"Who?"

"Nathan Johnson. The boy I saw the other night. That's him. Oh my god. Can you print this for me?"

"Sure I can, sweetie."

"I can't believe this happened in our fucking house."

"And they didn't bother to tell you, that's illegal you know. I would be pissed off too."

"No wonder it was so damn cheap. Our realtor will be hearing from me. You can count on that."

"Do you think that psychopath could have escaped from prison?" Crystal asked.

"I fucking hope not. If he did, I need to know about it."

"Let me look," Crystal said and typed in the murderer's name. Robert Collins had been institutionalized for life. As they read more, they learned that died of an intentional overdose. He had taken a bunch of prescription drugs he had managed to get while he was in the institution. His son Michael was sent to a foster home.

"This is too much. What if this guy's ghost is after Michael? His son was named Michael and maybe he's coming after my Michael now," said Tanya.

"Come on, Tanya. That's crazy," said Crystal.

"I know, but all of these night terrors and now this. I know what I saw, Crystal, and it was that boy Nathan."

"Maybe you guys should start looking for another house then."

"Ron loves the place, and he painted the nursery all special for the baby. He even redid the kitchen and put in a big pantry for me."

"Well, if ever you need anything or a place to stay I'm only a phone call away."

"Thank you, Crystal. You're the best friend ever," said Tanya and gave her a hug.

"I have just the thing to cheer you up," said Crystal reaching into her fridge.

"Oh yeah? What's that?"

"Cheesecake," she replied and pulled out a fresh baked one.

"You really are the best. Thanks again."

"Don't mention it," she said and cut them both a slice.

*****

Michael was late getting home that day. Tanya waited an hour, but he did not show up. She paced, wondering where he was. She called the school and the receptionist answered. Tanya asked if they had seen him leave. "One of the teachers said he got a ride with Phillip's mom," said the receptionist.

"That's right. He said he was going to Phillip's house after school. Thank you," she told the receptionist and hung up the phone. Minutes later the phone rang.

An older sounding woman asked, "Is Tanya there?"

"May I ask who this is?"

"Yes. This is Sandra, Phillip's mom."

"Oh, hello, I'm Michael's mom, Tanya. Is he with you now?"

"Yes, he's here. I was just letting you know I picked him up from school. What good manners he has."

Tanya sighed with relief.

"Well that is good to hear. Thank you so much for picking him up."

"No problem. He wants to ask you something," she said. "Hold on just a minute."

"Hi, Mom, can I stay the night at Phillip's tonight? Please?" Michael asked.

"I don't have a problem with that. Is it okay with his mom?"

"He said it was, and she gave her permission."

"I want you to promise me you will be on your best behavior and use your manners while you are over there."

"Okay Mom. I promise I will."

"I love you."

"I love you too, Mom"

"Can I speak with Sandra now?" she asked, putting her hand on her hip.

"Sure," he said.

"Hello," Sandra said.

"Is that all right with you if Michael stays over?" Tanya asked.

"Sure. What time do you want to come and get him tomorrow?"

"Around 10 a.m. if that works for you."

"10 a.m. will be fine."

"I look forward to meeting you," said Tanya.

"So do I," Sandra said and hung up the phone.

When Ron got home, Tanya explained to him what had happened in their home nearly twenty years ago.

"Please tell me you're joking," he said, eyes wide open.

"Does it sound like I'm joking?" She handed him the article she had printed at Crystal's house.

"That fucking bitch. Why didn't she tell us about this when we moved in here?" he said, slamming the article down on the table. "Don't you think we have a right to know these things?"

"Yes. I absolutely do. That's why I'm going to call her tomorrow and see if she can find us a better place."

Ron squinted. "I've put a lot of work into this place. I'm not about to give it up just like that. I mean even if we got a refund we wouldn't find a place nearly as good as this for 200k."

"Three kids were murdered here by some psychopath for Christ's sake. I'm not about to let our son be terrorized by their ghosts."

"For fuck sake, Tanya, that's crazy. Don't tell me you believe that shit."

"I believe what I saw, and what I saw is this boy right here." Tanya put the paper up to Ron's face and pointed at one of the pictures. "His name was Nathan Johnson and he was one of the victims. I saw the same kid but without--"

"What, was he missing his eyes?" said Ron sarcastically.

"How can you not take me seriously right now?"

"Because this is too fucking crazy to believe, that's how."

"What about Michael? He said he saw the same boy I did, and the boy's head in his bed. The article says all three boys had been dismembered and mutilated."

Ron's mouth opened wide as he put his hand on his head. "So where is this guy now?"

"He's dead."

"Well that's reassuring."

"Not really. What if his ghost has come back for Michael? His son's name was Mike too."

"So he murdered his own son?"

"No. He was the only one to survive. They found him hiding in a tree scared to death."

Ron opened held out his palms and tilted his head in confusion. "So what happened to him?"

"I'm not sure. He was put into foster care. That's all it says."

"Well, the guy is dead. There is no way his ghost is here," said Ron.

"What about the figure?" Tanya said. The baby kicked as fear grew in her stomach.

"You have got to knock this shit off, Tanya. We're all okay. No one is hurt."

"What about Tigger? Michael claimed he saw the monster."

"Maybe I should take you to see Dr. Donahue."

Tanya's eyebrows furrowed and her lips puckered out.

"Fuck you," said Tanya and punched him in the arm.

"What the hell was that for?"

"Tigger scratched the hell out of our son and has been missing since last night, you asshole."

She threw the article on the floor by the bar and stormed out of the room.

"I'm sorry. How in the hell was I supposed to know that?" Ron bellowed.

*****

Michael had been playing Knights of the Round Table with Phillip for hours. Phillip had two wooden swords and shields his mom had bought for him at the Renaissance Fair. Phillip was King Arthur, Michael was Lancelot, and they were after a dragon. Phillip had attached a red dragon mask to some bales of hay with a red blanket over them. They attacked it, and Phillip chopped off the dragon's head and held his sword high in the air.

"I killed the dragon," he proclaimed.

"That dragon isn't scary at all," said Michael. "There's a real monster living in my dresser," said Michael.

Phillip stared at Michael as if sand crabs were crawling out of his ears.

"Yeah, right," said Phillip, throwing the dragon mask at Michael.

Michael caught it. "Want to make a bet?"

"Yeah. I bet you that sword and shield that you're lying."

"Deal." Michael spun the sword in the air and caught it by the handle.

"So what's this monster looked like?"

"He's black with sharp claws and fangs and the scariest eyes you've ever seen."

"Is he big?"

"Yep. He's tall and smelly and super scary."

"You're bullshitting me," said Phillip. He shook his head and swung his sword at Michael. Michael blocked it with his shield.

"I swear," said Michael, and stabbed Phillip.

"Ouch. That hurt, fucker"

"You're a wimp."

"Screw you. When can I see it?"

Michael thought for a moment. "Next weekend is my birthday. I'll ask my mom if you can stay the night then."

"Okay, but I still think you're a fucking liar."

"Just wait. You'll see."

Phillip attacked Michael with his wooden scimitar but Michael stepped to the side, dodging the attack. Michael countered, hitting Phillip in the back of his legs and bringing him to his knees.

"I got you," said Michael as he pointed his sword inches away from Phillip's throat.

"Beginners luck," said Phillip.

Sandra called them for dinner.

"Be there in a minute," Phillip yelled. "For fuck sake," he said under his breath.

"You shouldn't talk like that to your mom."

"She didn't hear me, you goober." Phillip dropped his sword and shield, and took off running. "Last one inside is a stinky fart," he called. Michael held his sword and shield, and raced to the door. Phillip beat him. "I win, you stinky fart."

"Cause you cheated," said Michael.

*****

That night, Ron spoke to Tanya.

"I'm sorry about what I said earlier, babe. I really didn't mean what I said about you seeing Dr. Donahue. It was wrong of me."

"It's okay. After everything that has happened here it probably wouldn't hurt," said Tanya.

"I can't believe the awful things that have happened here. I know you and the baby have been through a lot these past couple of nights and so I . . ."

"So you what?"

He wrapped his arms around her and whispered in her ear. "I made us reservations to see 'A Midsummer Night's Dream' tomorrow night."

"Wow, I don't know what to say," she said.

"How about 'thank you'?"

"Thank you so much," she said and kissed his cheek. "Oh. What about Michael?"

"Taken care of—I hired a babysitter from an agency called We Care."

"You should have told me. I could have had him stay with Crystal."

"He'll be fine. It's not like we'll be gone all night."

She nodded. "You're right."

"I got a nice Merlot for us too." He uncorked the bottle of Ravenswood and got them two crystal glasses from behind the bar.

"You must have read my mind. Ravenswood is my favorite."

"I know." Ron poured the wine. "Here's to my beautiful wife, who makes for our family a beautiful life."

*****

The next day Tanya picked Michael up at 10 a.m. sharp. He ran to her and wrapped his arms around her waist. "Can Phillip stay at our house next Friday since it's my birthday on Saturday?"

"We'll see."

"But Phillip's mom already said it was okay. Please." He put his hands together as if he were praying.

"I said we'll see."

"Okay fine," said Michael. His shoulders and head drooped. He walked back up to the porch to grab his bag of clothes. "See you at school, Phillip."

"See you later masturbator," said Phillip quietly.

"Watch your mouth, Phillip Gibbons," Sandra said.

At home, Tanya told Michael that she and Ron were going out for the night and that he would have a babysitter. "No Mom. Why?" Michael whined.

"Your dad surprised me last night with tickets to see a play mommy has wanted to see for a while! Can I count on you to be brave and look after the house?"

"What if the monster comes?"

"I promise no monster will come."

"Please don't leave me here."

"You won't be alone. And I promise that as soon as the play is over we will come straight home."

"I'm scared," he said.

"Honey, I promise you nothing will happen. I'm going to leave you my pager number, so if you feel frightened you can page me, and I will call you back."

"You swear?"

"Yes I swear. Do this for Mommy and I will let Phillip stay over next Friday."

"You promise?"

"I promise."

"All night?"

"Yes, he can stay all night, sweetie."

"Do you pinky promise?"

"Yes, I pinky promise," said Tanya and grabbed his pinky with hers.

# Chapter 6 The Babysitter

Around 7 p.m., the doorbell rang, and Ron answered it. A short older lady was standing outside the door. "Hi. My name is Gloria, and I am from We Care," she said, shaking Ron's hand.

"Hi, Gloria, my name is Ron. It's a pleasure to meet you."

Tanya came down the stairs. "You two look stunning," said Gloria, admiring Tanya's green dress and Ron's gray dress shirt and black suit.

"Well thank you," said Tanya and introduced herself. "His bedtime is 10:00," Tanya told her.

"Be good for her, buddy," Ron told Michael and rubbed his head.

"I will," said Michael smiling.

Tanya gave him a hug and a kiss. "She seems nice, sweetie. Here. Take this." She handed Michael a piece of paper with her pager number on it. "I only want you to page me if it's an emergency, not if you have a bad dream. Okay?"

He nodded and gave her another hug. "I love you," he said and put Tanya's pager number into his pocket.

"I love you, son. Be good now. You're the man of the house until I get back," Ron said.

"I love you too, Dad. I will."

"You two have a great time, and don't worry about anything," said Gloria.

"So Michael, do you like cookies?"

"Uh-uh," said Michael nodding his head with a smile.

"What is your favorite?"

"Chocolate chip."

"What do you say we make some then?"

"Okay." Michael ran into the kitchen, anxious to lend a hand. He helped her mix the dough, and Gloria let him lick the bowl when they were finished. After that, Gloria brought the cookies into the TV room.

"My dad would ground me if he saw me eating cookies on his black leather couch."

"Oh, we should probably eat them in the kitchen then," said Gloria picking up the plate of cookies. After they finished eating, they went back into the TV room and The Golden Girls. Michael grew bored quickly and talked her into letting him watch Goosebumps.

"This show is actually pretty good. Your Mom doesn't mind you watching this sort of thing?" asked Gloria.

"No, she lets me watch it."

After watching Goosebumps for a bit, Michael excused himself to the bathroom, and he found some papers on the floor by the bar on the way to the bathroom. When he got to the bathroom he looked them over, and there on the front page was the same drunk man he had seen in his dream. He flipped through the other pages and saw the three boys from his dream. Frightened, he threw the article in the wastebasket.

At 10 Michael brushed his teeth and changed into his pajamas, pulling his mom's pager number from his pants and putting it in the pocket of his pajamas. "Goodnight. Don't let the bed bugs bite," Gloria said as she tucked him in.

"Goodnight," Michael said. He lay in his bed trying to think of anything but the monster. He thought of playing with Phillip and being a real knight saving a beautiful princess from a fire-breathing dragon. Soon he fell asleep.

Gloria watched X-Files downstairs. It was starting to rain heavily. There were loud cracks of thunder and bright flashes of lightning. The television started to cut out. "What is this?" she said. The television turned off. "What the hell is this?" she said and pushed the power button on the controller. Nothing happened so she got up close to the TV and pushed the power button on the monitor. Still nothing. She checked to see if it was plugged in and it was. "Must be this damn weather," she said. She hit the side of the TV with her hand and the top of it with her fist. As her fist struck it, the glass screen exploded embedding glass in her face and arms. She screamed and fell to the ground just as thunder and lightning struck. A growl came from inside the television. She scooted backwards on her butt toward the couch and stood just as the Black Monster emerged from it and grabbed her head. It twisted it off, and her lifeless body fell onto the couch, blood pouring from her headless neck. The foul monster threw her severed head inside the television and vanished back into the couch, taking Gloria's body with him. The broken glass from the shattered screen came back together like pieces of a huge puzzle, slowly covering Gloria's severed head. The blood was absorbed back into the couch, the television turned back on, and X-Files started to play again.

*****

Michael woke to the sound of Tigger meowing somewhere in his room. A scratching sound came from the hole in his wall that Ron had made with the baseball bat. He carefully got up from his bed to investigate. He heard Tigger meow again from inside the wall. "Is that you, boy? How did you get in there?" He approached the hole and up popped Tigger's head. "There you are, boy. I was worried sick about you," said Michael as he reached to grab him. Michael saw the monster holding Tigger's severed head in his long claws as his entire arm emerged from the dark hole in the wall. The monster let go of the head and quickly grabbed Michael's arm through the hole in the wall as Tigger's decapitated head fell to the floor. He screamed out, as the creature broke free from the wall. It picked Michael up by his arm and meowed. Michael screamed again at the top of his lungs and the creature let out a hellish growl.

Michael woke, sweating profusely. He ran to his parent's room and yanked open the door, but they were not home yet. He ran down the stairs, screaming for

Gloria. She wasn't on the couch, but the TV was on. He checked the bathroom, but she wasn't there either. He grabbed the piece of paper with Tanya's pager number on it and picked up the phone to call his mom. There was no dial tone. Someone breathed on the other end.

"Gloria?" he asked.

"Leave the house now," a boy's voice said.

Michael heard the same growl he had just heard in his dream. It came from upstairs. He screamed and dropped the phone and ran for the front door. Before he reached the door, he looked to his left and saw the monster crawling down the stairs on all fours. He hurried outside into the rain, slamming the door shut behind him. He ran to Gloria's car parked out front and tried to open the driver's side door, but it was locked. He ran to the passenger's side, but it was also locked. He yelled for help, but thunder drowned out his voice. Lightning struck, and the neighborhood went dark. Michael's legs shook and then buckled. He fell to his knees crying for his mom. He lifted his head and noticed a large puddle a few feet in front of him. Bubbles rose from the murky black water then stopped. A bullfrog emerged from it and hopped off into the woods.

Michael stood and as he turned to walk toward the house, the black creature jumped out from the puddle and pulled him to the ground by his foot. He screamed and pulled away from the creature as hard as he could. His sock slipped off into the monster's hand. He got to his feet and ran as fast as he could back to the house with the creature following.

When Michael reached his house, he found the front door locked. The monster was just a few feet behind him and it would most certainly get him if he didn't move fast. He ran into the woods, crying for help. He followed the trail to a tree. He stopped to catch his breath. He turned his head to see lightning flash behind him. He jumped out of the way and landed on his back as the creature reached for him.

Someone called his name in a soft calm voice. When he looked up, an ethereal woman was signaling him with her hand to follow her. He followed her and she led him to a giant tree. When Michael reached the tree, the woman was gone. The creature was advancing so he climbed the tree until he reached a large limb where the monster could not reach him.

The monster was a good seven feet from the tree when suddenly it stopped and let out a loud hissing roar before disappearing into the ground. Michael started to cry and seconds later, the thunder and lightning ceased and the rain died down. A soft peaceful voice said, "Rest my child." He lay down on the limb and listened to the crickets and bullfrogs. He tried to relax and, before long, he was asleep.

*****

Tanya was having the time of her life with Ron at the play. They had a wonderful dinner and the theater was enormous. Once the play ended, she told Ron she wanted to get back home to check on Michael.

"Ok, honey," he said. "Did you enjoy it?"

"This was the most amazing thing anyone has ever done for me," she said. "I love you so much. Thank you."

"You're welcome, babe. To see you enjoying yourself gives me more joy than anything else," he said and gave her a kiss. "Now let's go home."

*****

Michael dreamed about a little girl playing on a swing in the same tree he was sleeping in. The beauty of the place amazed him. When the little girl looked up from the swing, she saw an angel high in the tree looking down at her smiling. The little girl jumped off the swing and started to climb the tree. Once she reached the branch with the angel, she lost her footing and fell.

Before she hit the ground, the angel caught her. He looked down at her smiling and she looked up at him and asked him what his name was.

"I am the archangel Michael," he replied with a smile. He put a gold chain with a withered gold medallion on it around her neck and told her, "Whenever you need me, recite this prayer and I will aide you. 'Most powerful of angels, protect me from harm.'" He told her that as long as she wore the medallion, it would protect her from harm.

She looked at him and said, "I love you, Michael."

"I love you too, Maya," he said with a smile. He put her down gently and vanished. Michael watched as the girl continued to swing.

# Chapter 7 Sheriff Wilson

When Ron and Tanya got home the television was on and a very bad smell was coming from somewhere within the house. Tanya's heart raced as she remembered that same smell in Michael's room.

"Gloria, we're back," Tanya yelled, but no one answered.

"Gloria, we're back," yelled Ron, but no one answered. "I'll check the bathroom." He returned seconds later. "It's empty."

They walked upstairs and saw that Michael was not in his bed. Ron yelled for him but got no answer. He searched the entire house but didn't find him.

"Where the hell could they have gone?" Tanya yelled.

"Not far. Gloria's cars parked right outside."

"Something doesn't feel right, Ron. I think we should call the police.

While they waited for the police, Ron went out back to see if they might be outside while Tanya searched for where the smell was coming from. It seemed to be coming from Ron's black leather couch, and when Tanya looked closely, she noticed more of the stinky slimy stuff on it.

She quickly cleaned up the mess. Ron came through the sliding glass door.

"They're not out back. I'm going to check the garage."

Tanya paced and thought about the monster. "What if Michael was right?" she said to Ron when he returned. "God, Ron. I'm so scared."

He cupped her head in his hand and pulled her head to his chest then wrapped his other arm around her as her tears trickled down his shirt.

A loud knock at the door caused Tanya to jump.

"Honey, look at me. It will be okay," said Ron. He opened the door to a tall policeman in a cowboy hat.

"Howdy. I'm Sheriff Wilson, and you must be Tanya." He tipped his hat and winked at her.

"And I am Ron, her husband." Ron shook his hand firmly.

Tanya's was panicked and frightened. Her heart was palpitating. She began to sweat when he arrived. "Something bad has happened to our son," she said.

"Come inside," said Ron leading him to the sofa.

"What in god's name is that horrible smell?" asked Sheriff Wilson.

"We are not sure ourselves. It was here when we got home," said Ron.

Tanya shook and cried heavily.

"Relax Tanya. Chances are your son is okay. How old is Michael?"

"He is only eight years old."

"Has he ever wandered off late at night before?"

"No never."

"What can you tell me about the babysitter?"

"Her name is Gloria. She was in her sixties. She worked for an agency called We Care."

"What time did she arrive at your home?"

"Around 7 p.m. When we got home they were both gone."

"What time did you arrive home?"

"Half past midnight."

"I'm scared. What if something bad has happened to Michael?" said Tanya crying.

"Don't worry, babe. He's okay," said Ron.

"How the fuck do you know that? I mean Gloria's car is still parked right outside." Sheriff Wilson tipped his hat and excused himself. He stepped outside to look at Gloria's car. He turned on his flashlight and looked through the car window. Her purse was still there. He opened the door and looked through her purse then grabbed her wallet and a directory of numbers she kept in her purse.

"Mrs. Walker, chances are an older lady with a little boy wouldn't get very far without her car."

"Could you please look for my boy, sheriff? Please?"

"Okay, well I will send out a unit to search for him and Gloria and, hopefully, they will find them both soon," said Sheriff Wilson "I also need to know, does your son have any behavioral problems or mental issues like schizophrenia or bipolar disorder? Anything like that?"

"No, nothing like that. He's a good kid," said Tanya.

"Okay then I will dispatch a unit to start the search now," said Sheriff Wilson as he opened the front door to leave. "I will drop by tomorrow at around noon regardless," he said.

"Okay, thank you, sheriff," said Tanya as he left.

She and Ron searched the entire neighborhood for Michael and Gloria but they did not find them. Tanya drove around searching for them while Ron searched the neighborhood on foot.

She drove to the big rock where she took him right after they moved into their home but they weren't there. She drove to the pond where they caught tadpoles a couple of weeks earlier but neither of them were there either. She saw a police car with its searchlights on and pulled up next to it. She rolled down her window. "Are you searching for my son?" she asked.

"Ma'am, can you tell me your son's name?"

"Michael Walker. He is eight years old, brown hair, brown eyes."

"You're Mrs. Walker then?" asked the officer.

"Yes, I am Mrs. Walker."

"I haven't had much luck, but I will keep looking."

"Thank you. God, I hope you find him." She searched until a quarter 'til three. She was crying and exhausted. When she got home, she sat in her car trying to think of where he might be.

"Please, God. Let my son be safe. Watch over him, Lord and see that he returns safely to me. I beg you, please." She dozed off.

*****

When Michael awoke, the sun was just starting to come up. He climbed down from the tree. Just like in his dream, many varieties of beautiful wildflowers surrounded the tree. It was truly the most serene place he had ever seen. He didn't want to leave, but he knew his parents must be worried sick about him, so he ran home. His mom answered the door.

Tanya collapsed to her knees and hugged him crying. "God I am so glad you're okay," she said in a shaky voice.

"We were worried sick, slugger," said Ron as he came up behind Tanya and picked Michael up into the air for a hug.

"I bet you're hungry. Would you like me to make you some scrambled eggs?" said Tanya.

"Yes please. I am starving," said Michael. After Michael ate his eggs, Tanya took a seat next to him at the kitchen table and gave him a serious look.

"Where were you all night?" Tanya asked him.

"The monster chased me outside and into the forest. I slept in a tree where he couldn't get me." Ron grabbed him firmly by the arm.

"I'm tired of you lying to us about this fucking monster. Where is Gloria? Did you scare her away with all this monster talk?"

"I don't know where she is, Dad. I swear! When I woke up, she was gone. I looked for her but she wasn't in the house."

"So you're telling me she just up and left?" He threw his arms into the air.

"I don't know, Dad. I swear." Michael shook his head back and forth.

"We had the police searching for you and for Gloria all fucking night. I need the truth. Now. What the hell happened after we left?"

"Gloria baked me cookies, and we watched some television."

"Then what?" he asked.

"Then I went to the bathroom and found a piece of paper with Mike's dad being put into a cop car."

"What did you just say?" asked Tanya.

"It was Mike's drunk dad in the picture."

"How do you know about Mike?" she asked.

"He probably read the article," said Ron.

"No. I saw him in my dream."

Ron went to slap him, but he stopped himself. "When are you going to stop fucking lying to us?"

"Don't touch him, Ron! What if he is telling the truth?"

"I won't hit him, but come on—a monster, Tanya, really? You're grounded, Michael. Until you can start telling the truth," he yelled. "I'm going to call the agency and see if they have heard from Gloria."

Tanya got on her knees and took Michael in her arms. She kissed his cheek and wiped away his tears.

Tanya said, "Baby, I love you, and I want to believe you, but your dad is right. We need to know exactly what happened."

"I had a bad dream about the monster killing Tigger," he said. "When I woke up I thought you were home, but you weren't, so I yelled for Gloria, but she left me."

"Do you know where she went, honey?" She stroked his hair.

"I swear I don't know," he said as he started to cry.

Tanya gave him a hug. "It's ok, baby. We will figure this out. What happened after you saw that she was gone?"

"I picked up the phone to page you but a boy answered and told me to leave the house. That's when I heard it."

"Heard what, honey?"

"The black monster."

"The house smelled bad when we got home last night," Tanya said. "It was the same smell in your bedroom yesterday. When I searched for where the smell was coming from, the couch had more of the same black nasty smelling slime on it that I found on your dresser. Do you swear to me that you were not playing with that stinky slime on the couch last night?"

"It was from the monster. I swear to you, Mom. He came down the stairs, so I ran outside to get help. And when I did it came out of a black puddle and grabbed my foot. It even pulled off my sock."

"Did this monster look anything like Mike's dad? The man you saw in the newspaper article?"

"No. It's black with eyes like blood and long sharp pointy teeth. It's so scary." He started to cry. "I want to move, Mommy," he said as he leaned forward and hugged her waist, squeezing her as tears ran down his cheeks.

"It's all right, baby. Mommy does too. We just have to find a new place first. But, honey, if you know where Gloria went, I need you to tell me now. I promise I won't get upset."

"She was watching television on the couch where you found the slime. Maybe the monster took her."

"Took her where, sweetie?"

Before Michael could answer, Ron came back in the room.

"So have they heard anything from Gloria?" Tanya asked.

"Nothing at all. They told me to call them once we know something. Are you ready to tell the truth now?" he asked Michael.

"I told Mom the truth. She knows everything," he said.

"Ok. So tell me now."

"Why don't you ask her?"

"Okay Tanya. Where is the monster?"

"Stop acting like an asshole."

"I'm an asshole? Our son is out all night and has no recollection of where in the hell the babysitter might be. And the best answer he can come up with is that a real monster is after him. And where in the fuck is that awful smell coming from?"

"It's the monster," said Tanya smiling. Michael smiled too.

"Well you can tell the police that when they come back here," Ron yelled as he stormed off. Tanya asked Michael more about the dream he had with Mike's dad in it.

"Mike was in his bedroom where the three boys from the newspaper were. They were jumping up and down on the bed. The creature killed all three of them then went after Mike as he hid inside of the closet. I woke up before it got him.

"So what about Mike's dad?"

"I saw Mike's dad asleep in the same room where dad and you sleep. He was asleep the whole time."

"So you're saying he did not kill the kids."

"I swear the monster did."

"Okay honey. I believe you."

"You do?"

"Well about your dream, yes. About a monster, I'm not sure. But I don't think we're safe in this house. I have to try to convince your father to sell the place. And that could take some time. Now the cops are going to come over and ask you some questions, and I don't want you telling them about the monster. I want you to tell them you went looking for Gloria and that you walked to Crystal's house. That is where you were last night. OK, sweetie?"

"Okay."

"I need you to pinky promise Mommy now."

"I pinky promise," he said, and Tanya gave him a kiss.

"Do you remember how to get to Crystal's house from here?"

"Sort of," he said to her.

"Okay, can you show me if I got in my car."

"I think so," said Michael. He had been to Crystal's house at least a dozen times with Tanya and another dozen times by himself since he moved, and he had a good sense of direction. Tanya and Michael got into her Honda Accord, and she had Michael direct her on how to get to Crystal's. He showed her exactly how to get there from his house.

"I am impressed. You pay good attention when I drive, don't you?"

"Uh huh." Michael nodded his head.

"It would be good if you could pay attention like that in school too, mister," said Tanya.

She told him to remember that route in case the cops asked him.

She knocked on Crystal's door about 8:30 with Michael's pajamas in her hand.

"Hey, sweetie, something is wrong. I can tell. Come inside I'll make us some coffee."

Tanya and Michael followed Crystal inside and they both took a seat at the kitchen table. "What's going on?"

"The monster almost got me last night," said Michael.

Crystal's eyes widened.

"Honey, could you do Mommy a favor and wait in the other room for a bit?" said Tanya.

"Can I look at your crystals, Crystal?" Michael asked.

"Sure sweetie. You know where they are. Just be careful with them."

Crystal had taught Michael about her precious stones. He knew that quartz crystal had healing powers and loved the patterns on the Tiger's Eye. He grabbed an amethyst geode and gazed at it in wonder as if it were alive. Each new stone or crystal he picked up he would study thoroughly. They helped calm him but he found one he didn't like much. It was black like the monster and it made him uneasy. After he looked over all of them, he put them back one by one. His favorite was the aqua aura. Its pale blue color was mesmerizing, and when he held it his fears went away. He held it and studied it for nearly an hour. Tanya and Crystal came back into the room.

"What you got there?" asked Tanya.

Crystal replied, "One of my favorites."

"It's my favorite one too," said Michael with a big smile.

"You know aqua aura has some pretty special powers," said Crystal.

"Like what?"

"It can help one both speak and see the truth."

"What else?"

"It can help protect against parasitic or any other draining negative energies."

"Like the monster."

"Yeah, like the monster. It can also bring success and wealth."

"Can I keep it, Crystal? Please can I?"

"Yes. I think it would help you."

"Thank you so much, Crystal." He squeezed his arms around her waist with a smile from cheek to cheek.

"You know there is another one that I think will help you as well," said Crystal.

"What one?" Michael said.

Crystal picked up the black obsidian and handed it to Michael.

"I don't like that one. It reminds me of the monster."

"You shouldn't be afraid, Michael. Black obsidian is a spiritual protector. It helps one understand and face their deepest fears."

"Like the monster."

"Yes."

"You are the best, you know that?" said Tanya to Crystal.

"I love you both dearly, you know that?"

"Yes I do. Thank you so much."

"You are always welcome."

"Well we should get going. It's nearly eleven, and Sheriff Wilson said he would come by at noon."

"Okay sweetie. Good luck and I hope Ron simmers down."

"I hope so too."

*****

Once they arrived back at the house, Tanya covered the hole in Michael's wall with a poster from one of his magazines then sprayed Lysol throughout the house and lit some candles. She lifted up the black leather cushions of Ron's couch to see if any more of the black slime was there, but everything seemed normal. An hour later Sheriff Wilson stopped by. Michael looked up at him as if he were the lone ranger.

"Wow is that a real gun?" asked Michael as he stared wide eyed at Sheriff Wilson's Colt Peacekeeper.

"It sure is."

Tanya invited him in. Ron came downstairs to greet him.

"So you must be Michael. It is good to see that you are home. Where in the hell have you been all this time, Michael?"

"He was at my best friend Crystal's house," said Tanya.

"Ma'am, if I wanted you to answer, I would have addressed you. I want to hear it from him."

"I'm sorry."

"Now tell me, boy. Where were you all night?"

"I walked to Crystal's house."

"In the pouring rain . . . What would possess you to do that when you have a nice cozy warm home, and your parents were going to be home soon?"

"I was scared."

"Yeah, well I would be scared too if I was eight, and the babysitter left me alone. Did you try and look for her, Michael?"

"I couldn't find her."

"So why did you choose to go to Crystal's house?"

"She has some cool rocks."

"What is that supposed to mean?"

"She collects crystals and stones," said Tanya.

"Not another word. Do you hear me?" yelled Sheriff Wilson.

"Don't yell at her," said Ron.

"You sit down too. I am asking Michael the questions here. I don't need you two interfering with this investigation."

Ron took a seat on the couch next to Tanya.

"Can you tell me where Gloria is, Michael?"

"She was gone when I woke up."

"Say, have you or your husband heard anything from Gloria?"

"No. I tried calling the agency, and they haven't heard from her either," said Ron.

"Okay, Michael. So you woke up, and the babysitter was gone. Did she say where she was going?"

"No. She was gone when I walked downstairs."

"You know this is now a missing person's case, and you could get into big trouble for withholding information from me."

"I swear to you I don't know where she is."

"Do you mind if I take a look around?" the sheriff asked Tanya.

"Sure, go on ahead," said Ron.

He searched the house but found nothing. "Can you show me where Crystal lives?" he asked Michael.

"Yes, I can show you."

"Ma'am, I am going to need you to come along with me."

"What about me?"

"You stay here," said Sheriff Wilson.

"Please let me know if you find out anything, or when you have found Gloria," said Ron.

"I will."

Michael directed him right to Crystal's house. Sheriff Wilson knocked on the door. When she answered, he cleared his throat and fixed his eyes on her breasts, as her cleavage was showing a bit, so she quickly covered herself with her flannel sweater. "I'm Sheriff Wilson. You must be Crystal."

"Yes," she said.

"Hi sweetie," she said to Michael.

Before Michael could say hi back, the sheriff asked Crystal if she could tell him what happened last night.

"Michael came here panicked and wet around 1 a.m. so I ran him a hot bath, and after that I let him sleep in my guest bedroom."

"Do you mind if I take a look around?"

"No, not at all," said Crystal.

"Can I use your bathroom, Crystal?" asked Michael.

"Sure sweetie, you know where it is."

As Sheriff Wilson passed Crystal, his baton pushed into her side rather hard. "You can touch my night stick anytime," he said. Crystal gave him a very angry look. He checked all the rooms. "By the looks of it someone stayed here last night, there's an unmade bed. Where are your manners, boy? She lets you stay here, and you can't even make your bed? My mom used to tell me the devil would sleep in my bed when I didn't make it. You wouldn't want that now would you?"

"No, Officer Wilson," said Michael.

"Go make that bed," he said to Michael.

"I can do it," said Crystal.

"So can he," Sheriff Wilson exclaimed.

Michael made the bed, and Crystal said, "I forgot to give you your pajamas. I washed them for you, because they were soaking wet last night."

"What a woman. Look at that boy. She let you stay here and washed your pajamas for you. Now what do you say?"

"Thank you, Crystal."

"You're welcome, sweetie. Is there anything else?"

"No that will be all unless you would like to have a cup of coffee with me sometime."

"I'm sorry. I just got out of a bad relationship," said Crystal.

"Well then, sweet cheeks, here is my card in case you change your mind," he said and handed her his card.

"Thank you," she said as she showed him to the door.

*****

Sheriff Wilson drove Michael and Tanya back home.

"I'll be in touch if anything develops. Call me if you hear anything from Gloria."

"I sure will," said Tanya, taking his business card.

After he left, Michael said, "He was mean, Mom!"

"I know, honey," she said. "You did a wonderful job, sweetie. Normally you would tell the truth to a policeman, but in this case, I don't want you talking to him about a monster. Do you understand?"

"Yes Mom. I think so."

She gave Michael a hug and told him that she loved him very much.

Ron was still frustrated as he couldn't get a straight answer out of Michael and he was pissed at the sheriff for yelling at Tanya. "I'm going to go get some rest," he told Tanya.

# Chapter 8 Mike Collin's Story

"Mom, can I go and play outside?" asked Michael.

"Ok, but I want you in by two and no later. Understand?" He looked at the clock and it was noon so that gave him two hours.

"Thanks, Mom. You're the best."

"I love you sweetie. And be careful out there."

"I will."

Tanya called Crystal. "How about I take you out for dinner next Saturday? My treat," she offered.

"Isn't Michael's birthday next weekend?" said Crystal.

"It is on Friday and I promised him that Phillip could stay over that night. But Saturday night I'm free. Ron said he was going to watch Michael and have some friends over to play cards."

"That sounds great," said Crystal.

"Thanks again for doing this for me."

"It was a pleasure. And because of that rude pervert of a policeman I would have done it for free."

"He was kind of a creep and really rude too. He yelled at me to take a seat and not interrupt him. Ron got pissed."

"What did Ron do?"

"He told him not to yell at me, so the sheriff told him to take a seat too while he asked Michael what happened."

"What a dick. He bumped into me with his baton and said I could touch his nightstick anytime."

"You've got to be kidding me."

"No, he was that bad."

"Well then I really owe you one. Thanks again."

"You don't owe me a thing, sweetie."

"I look forward to seeing you on Saturday. It will be fun just us two ladies."

"I can't wait."

"Me either. How about I come by around 7 p.m.?"

"Perfect. It will be a girl's night out," said Crystal.

"I will see you then."

After she hung up the phone, Tanya checked the mail. As usual, it was ads, coupons, and junk. As she threw some of it in the trashcan on the side of the house, a gust of wind came from out of nowhere and blew her mail everywhere. As she picked it all back up, she noticed a large puddle of black water. As she looked closer, she could see something floating in it. She grabbed a nearby stick and retrieved the floating object. It was one of Michael's socks covered in black slime. She brought the sock up to her nose and sure enough, it smelled just like the slime on Michael's dresser. She flung it into the trash and went inside to watch some television and relax.

*****

Michael was playing with a stick by the large tree he had slept in. He was pretending to fight the monster with it. The wind blew some tall grass to the side, revealing what appeared to be a headstone. Michael pulled away some of the grass and looked closer. The headstone read "Maya Anne Collins 1939-1976."

"She was my mother," said someone standing behind Michael. He turned to look and there stood a middle-aged man in a brown leather jacket, white shirt, and blue jeans. He had blue eyes and brown hair. "My name's Mike," he said as he shook Michael's hand.

"Yeah I know. My name's Mike, too."

"What a coincidence. It's nice to meet you," he said.

"It is nice to meet you, too."

"You sure have a strong hand shake. How did you know my name?"

"I dreamt about you the other night."

"Wow. That's pretty cool."

"So how did you escape it?"

"Escape what?"

"The black monster—how did you escape it?"

Mike's eyes widened as he looked over at Michael. "How did you know about that?"

"Because the same monster is after me."

That can't be," Mike muttered.

"It came for me last night and chased me into the woods. I think it killed my babysitter too. I'm scared. I don't know what to do. How did you escape when it grabbed you by your neck in the closet?"

"How could you possibly know that?"

"I had a bad dream, and I saw what happened to you and your friends. I see their ghosts in my house, and they tell me to leave."

Mike put his hand onto Michael's shoulder. "I'm so sorry you had to see that. They were my good friends from school. The Pavor Nocturnus murdered them in front of me."

"What is a Pa-vor -"

"Nocturnus?" finished Mike.

"Yeah, what is it?" asked Michael

"A night terror. A real one. He can materialize from anything black and dark, like a shadow or any object that might be painted black. A table or jacket. But if you paint the object white, it can't come out of it again. Now I don't want you to go around painting everything white and get into trouble with your parents, but I would tell them to get rid of anything black around the house that it might come out of. It worked for me for a bit."

"Why does it come out of black things?" asked Michael.

"It uses dark objects as a portal or gateway into this world."

"What world is it from?"

"A very dark one, absent of light I imagine."

"When did you first see it?"

"In a dream just after my mom died."

"I meant when did you really see it?"

"Well I remember it was raining hard outside that day. When I came inside from playing my dad gave me a plate of food. I ate really fast. He had me do my homework as it was getting late. I ran upstairs, took out my homework, and started working on it. I must have dozed off, because when I woke up it was nearly midnight. It was still raining pretty hard outside, and I heard thunder crash, and I saw lightning. I looked out the window and waited for lightning to strike again. And when it did I noticed a tall spooky dark figure standing in a puddle with a long black trench coat on holding a black umbrella. When lightning struck again, the figure was gone, but the coat was lying in the puddle so I grabbed my jacket, but my umbrella was missing. I ran outside, and that big trench coat was lying in the large black puddle. When I picked it up, I realized it was my dad's, but the thing wearing it wasn't my dad. The coat smelled really bad, and it was covered in slime so I threw it onto a chair on my porch and went back to my room. It was dark when I got upstairs, so I turned the hallway light on. When I entered my room, it was dark, so I turned on my lamp, but it didn't work so I tried to unscrew it, and I cut my finger on the broken light bulb. I wondered to myself how the light bulb got broken when suddenly my black umbrella opened up all on its own. It wasn't there a minute ago. It was still wet. So I reached to grab it, and Pavor Nocturnus came halfway out of it. He grabbed me by the sleeve of my jacket. I screamed. The monster roared, and I slipped out of my jacket and woke up my dad. I tried to tell him that I saw a monster, but he didn't believe me. No one did."

"Don't feel bad. No one believes me either," said Michael.

"I'm sorry you are burdened with this," said Mike. "My dad thought I was crazy, and he took me to see a Doctor Donahue."

"That is my doctor too," said Michael.

"I told you there was a reason for us meeting here. He tried to hypnotize me and give me medicine but it didn't work."

"It didn't work for me either," said Michael. "So did it ever go away and leave you alone?"

"Yeah, it kind of went away after I moved. It didn't follow me."

"How come?"

"Because that night you saw me in the closet, I think I hurt it with this." He pulled a medallion from his neck. "I said the Archangel Michael's prayer when the monster had my neck, and a force of light came shooting out of the medallion at the monster. It screamed out in pain and disappeared back into the jacket. I came out here and hid up in my mom's tree."

"I hid in that tree last night, and I think I saw your mom too. She led me to this tree, and when I climbed up it the monster left."

"Wow, Michael. That is amazing. My mom used to tell me when I was a kid that this tree is where the angels would gather. She always felt safe here. I also remember her telling me that evil could not reach me here. That's when she gave me this medallion. She said that--"

"That the Archangel Michael gave it to her," Michael said. "I saw it in my dream last night. She fell from this tree and was caught--"

"By an angel," Mike finished. "I don't think it was an accident you and I meeting. I think God wanted us to meet. I want you to have this medallion. It has protected me for years and you need it more than I do. But you must say the prayer for it to work."

Michael recited the prayer.

"I'm impressed," said Mike.

"How did your mom die?"

"In her sleep. She had a heart attack. Not long after that, my dad became an alcoholic. He and my mom were very close. He actually built the house you live in now for my mom all those years ago so she could be near that tree. It was her whole world. After she died he had her cremated and he sprinkled some of her ashes on the tree's branches."

"What did he do with the rest of her?"

"He buried her ashes at the foot of this magical tree and made this headstone for her. I fly out here once a year to pay my respects."

"So what did your dad do after your mom died?"

"He was angry and lost without her. He started drinking heavily after that. It was sad that he was blamed for the murders of my friends. I tried to convince the police that he didn't do it, but they didn't believe me."

"Why?"

"Because when the police found him he was holding an axe. But he was trying to protect me with it, because he knew something had killed my friends. I kept telling the police a monster did it. But they called my dad the monster and put him into an insane asylum where he killed himself. Pavor Nocturnus framed my dad for the murders of my friends. I used to have a German shepherd named Prince, and he knew when it was coming. One rainy night he was barking and scratching at the door to go outside. My dad told me to let him out, and when I did, I saw the monster pull him into the ground. I screamed and cried, and I tried to tell my dad that the monster took him, but he wouldn't believe me. He thought he ran away."

"I think he killed my cat Tigger," said Michael. "No one believes me either."

"My dad was no monster. I probably shouldn't be telling you all of this stuff."

"Don't worry. I know he was innocent. When did the monster come?"

"It seemed as though Pavor Nocturnus came almost right after my mother died."

"Do you think it killed her?"

"I hope not, although when my father found her dead he said she had a scared look on her face. But that's probably because she had a heart attack."

"She seemed like a really nice lady, plus she saved my life last night."

"I would love to be able to see her again like you did though."

"You might if you stay here long enough," said Michael with a smile.

"That would be something," Mike said with a big smile. "I want you to be careful Michael and your family too."

"They don't believe me about the monster, and every time I bring it up I get into trouble."

"Trust me, I know the feeling," said Mike.

"Can I call you if I see the monster?"

"I'm heading back to Maine tonight to be with my family. I have a son about your age back home. You don't have to be afraid though. I sense great strength in you. Just stay strong and remember that prayer and never take the talisman off."

"Don't worry, I won't."

"I hope to see you around sometime. Take this. It's my business card."

"What do you do?" asked Michael.

"I'm an author."

"Oh cool."

"Good luck, bud. I'm going to stay with my mom for a minute."

"Okay. Do you know what time it is?"

"Yeah, it's 1:52."

"I better get back inside," said Michael and waved goodbye to Mike. He went back home and found his mom fast asleep on the couch. He grabbed a large trash bag and went up to his room and put every black object and toy in it. He carried it down the stairs, tied it up tight, and put it in the big trashcan in the garage. He went back upstairs with another trash bag and did the same thing with all of his black clothing. He headed for his parents' room. Ron was snoring loudly. He put all of their black clothes into large trash bags and dragged them to the trashcans one by one until there were no more black clothes left in the house. As he carried the last of the trash bags into the garage, he noticed a few cans of white paint sitting on the shelf. Ron had used it to paint the baby's room and crib. Michael grabbed a can of white paint from the garage and a paintbrush. He painted both of his black dressers including the handles white. When he finished it, he said, "Ha, you can't come out of there now." He went back downstairs with the paint after putting the lid back on the can, and he put the brush back with the can on the shelf where he got it. When he went back inside, Tanya was preparing dinner. "Hi, sweetie, did you have fun outside?"

"Yes. And I met Mike Collins."

"I don't know when to believe you," she said.

"I swear, Mom. His mom's grave is in the woods not too far from here, and he is in from Maine now. If we hurry, he might still be there.

Tanya thought for a moment. "Okay. Show me."

Michael led her outside and down the path into the forest to the tree.

"Wow. This place is amazing," she said.

"He must have left, but he gave me this." Michael reached into his pocket and handed Tanya the business card.

She looked it over and handed it back to Michael. "Oh you weren't fibbing."

"I told you he was here."

"What did he say?"

"He said his dad built our house for his mom because she loved this tree so much."

"How sweet."

Michael told her everything Mike had told him. He did not tell her; however, about the medallion Mike gave him. He figured it best to keep it to himself. Although a lot of what Michael was telling Tanya was really hard to swallow. She believed him, as every time she or Ron accused him of lying. Some kind of evidence would always turn up that proved he was not.

An uneasy feeling began to grow in the pit of Tanya's stomach. "Honey, Mommy doesn't feel too well," she told

Michael. "Thank you for bringing me here and showing me this special place though."

"You're welcome Mom. I'm sorry you're not feeling good."

"It's ok honey. It's not you. I am going to start making dinner. Want to give me a hand?"

"Sure, Mom.

"Let's go," she said and held his hand as they walked back to the house.

When they got back to the house, Ron was up. "Where have you two been?" he asked.

"Michael was showing me something," Tanya said.

"I thought I said he was grounded," said Ron.

"Give him a break. He has been suffering through this more than you and I have. And you weren't the one who had to sleep in a tree all night in the rain because the babysitter forgot to lock the door after she decided to leave our scared . . . let me rephrase that . . . our terrified son alone all by himself all night."

"You know what? You're right. I'm sorry I wasn't there for you, slugger. That had to have been scary sleeping in some tree all night in the rain all by yourself. "Want to hit on the bag with me."

"I asked him to help me prepare dinner," said Tanya.

"Okay, good idea. How about after dinner?"

"Sure, Dad. That will be cool," he said.

"Ok, my little Tyson," he said to him, throwing slow motion punches at him.

Michael swung back a little faster and harder. "Oh oh," said Ron, covering up.

"All right, you two, that's enough," said Tanya.

"I'm telling you this kid could be a pro," said Ron. "Go help your mom with dinner, champ." Michael went into the kitchen. He grabbed Mike's business card out of his pocket and stuck it to the black fridge with a magnet then helped his mom stir the spaghetti while she prepared the sauce and made the garlic bread.

# **Chapter 9 Haunted**

After dinner, Ron showed Michael some new moves on the bag. He taught him a right and left hook, as well an uppercut. He taught him jabs as well as how to dodge and avoid attacks. In the kitchen, Tanya grabbed the trashcan and carried it out to the garage. When she lifted the lid, it was full of bags that were not there before. She opened one of them and saw that it was full of all her black garments.

"Damn it, Michael," she cried to herself. She carried all the bags upstairs and started hanging all of Ron's clothes and her clothes back in the closet. She grabbed the remaining bags that contained all of Michael's clothes and toys, and she brought them up to his room. When she entered Michael's room, she noticed right away that Michael had painted his dresser white. The room reeked of paint. "Damn it," she said. He had made a mess. She started to clean up the mess he left behind. Paint had dried into the carpet, so she used some scissors to cut it out, but it still looked bad, as a lot of it had dripped down onto the floor. She grabbed an old blue throw rug from the garage, and used it to cover up the stains then opened his window to air out the room. She shut the door and walked downstairs.

Ron and Michael were still outside. She decided to let them play for a bit longer as she cleaned up the kitchen and did the dishes. Not long after she was done, they came back inside, and they both went into the living room to watch Goosebumps the Werewolf of Fever Swamp together.

"I thought you told him he was not allowed to watch scary movies at night," she said.

"This is not scary at all," Michael said.

She looked to Ron for an answer.

"It's not that bad," he said.

"Okay, but bedtime in an hour," she said.

"Okay, Mom," he said with a smile. Tanya kissed his head and asked if they would like some popcorn.

"Yes, please," they said at the same time.

"Okay boys," she said laughing.

She grabbed some buttered popcorn out of the pantry and put it in the microwave. The microwave beeped when it was done, and when she opened the door she screamed. There before her was the severed head of Brandon Burckhart, one of the boys from the article she had read. The severed head spoke and said, "You're all in danger. Leave this place." She slammed the microwave door, and Ron entered the kitchen.

"What the fuck happened? Are you all right?" he asked.

"It's in there. It's in there," she cried as she pointed to the microwave.

"What is it?" He grabbed the microwave door handle.

"Don't open it, please," she said crying.

"It's nothing," he said and opened the door and grabbed the popcorn.

"I swear it was Brandon's head."

"For fuck sake, Tanya, there is no head in here." He pointed inside the microwave.

"I swear on your life, Ron. His head was just lying there, and it told me we are in danger. I don't want to stay in this house another night. I want you to sell this place. I don't feel safe here." She grabbed him crying.

"I believe you," said Michael grabbing his mom's hand.

"You're not helping, Michael. In fact, this is partially your fault for putting these ideas in her head in the first place," yelled Ron.

"How dare you," Tanya yelled, slapping Ron's face. "He is not lying. There is some dark force here, and I want to go. Can we leave? Please can you sell this place for me?"

He said, "I want you to calm down."

"I know what I just saw," said Tanya crying.

"Okay. I will contact the realtor tomorrow and see if I can sell it. But please, relax. There is nothing in there, and you're safe with me here."

"Okay," said Tanya squeezing onto him tightly.

"Can I sleep with you tonight, Mom and Dad?" asked Michael.

Before Ron could say no, Tanya said, "Sure sweetie."

"Let's go to bed," said Ron and walked with both of them up to the master bedroom. Michael slept between his mom and dad. Tanya took a Valium and lay back down. Ron was already asleep and not long after, Tanya fell into a deep sleep.

Michael reached for his medallion. He held it and said, "Most powerful of angels protect my family and I from harm." He closed his eyes and as he fell asleep, the medallion glowed bright for a second and then dimmed.

*****

The next day Michael got up and finished the rest of his math homework quickly.

"I don't want you to leave important things, especially homework, to the last minute anymore. Do we have a deal?" asked Tanya.

"Yes, Mom," he said. He got ready for school.

Ron called the realtor to see if he could get a refund on the house but Margaret, the lady who sold them the house, had been let go a few weeks back. Ron said, "That doesn't surprise me. Let me speak to whoever is in charge of things there."

"One minute please, sir."

Ron waited and got an answering machine.

"Yeah, hi, this is Ron Walker, and I recently purchased a home from Margaret. I understand she has been fired. I want to sell this house ASAP so start looking for some buyers. Before we bought this place, Margaret didn't bother to tell us that three children were brutally murdered here, and now their ghosts are really freaking out my wife and child. My number is 909-267-3448 and if I don't hear back from you, you will definitely hear back from me and my lawyer." He hung up the phone.

"Don't worry, honey. It will be all right. You'll see."

"Thank you, honey, but there is one more thing," said Tanya.

"What is it?" asked Ron."

"Michael is supposed to see Dr. Donahue today at 3pm and he wants to hypnotize him. What do you think?"

"I guess I'm okay with it. We might get some real answers, just as long as he doesn't put him on any more medications."

"Okay. It's settled."

"If you need me for anything, beep me," he said giving her a kiss goodbye.

Michael grabbed his backpack and gave his mom a kiss and hug. "Honey, I will be picking you up after school today because we have a 3pm appointment with Dr. Donahue."

"Do I have to, Mom?" he said.

"Yes, you do so don't take the bus."

"Okay, Mom. I will wait for you," he said. He left for school. Ron waved bye to Michael from his work truck that was now running much better after he fixed the transmission. Tanya was still worried after what she saw last night, but she was also happy that Michael finally got a full night's rest for the first time in weeks. She felt rested too.

She took a hot shower and as she was doing her hair, the phone rang. She ran downstairs and into the kitchen and picked it up. "Hello," she said.

"May I please speak to Ron?"

"He isn't in right now. May I ask who this?"

"Yes, this is Sean, and I am the manager over here at Century 21. Do you know when he will be back?" he asked.

"Later this evening, but this is his wife Tanya. Are you having any luck finding us a new place?"

"Yes ma'am, but first off let me apologize for Margaret not telling you about the murders. That goes against our code not to mention the law, and I am so sorry for that.

But I assure you that you will get the same exact size home with the same amount of rooms and space. And I promise you that it won't have any bad history."

"Yeah things have been really spooky here, and I would like to move as soon as possible."

"I want to show you and your husband some nice two story homes, even today if you aren't busy."

"Actually today won't work as Michael has a doctor's appointment at 3, but I can ask Ron if he can take some time off tomorrow so that you can show us then maybe."

"That sounds great. Let me give you my pager number in case you or your husband might have any other questions for me."

Sean gave Tanya his pager number and work number as well, and apologized again for Margaret's inexcusable behavior. He assured her that by next week they would have a new home."

"Thank you for doing this, Sean. It means a lot to me."

"No problem at all, Mrs. Walker."

"You can call me Tanya."

"No problem, Tanya. I just want you and your husband to feel safe and comfortable in your new home."

"Thanks again. I wish I could have dealt with you to begin with and not Margaret."

"Trust me, I do too," he said, "but everything will be fine now."

"God I hope so," she muttered under her breath.

"Well Tanya, you have yourself a wonderful day, and I look forward to seeing you hopefully tomorrow."

"You too. Bye." She hung up the phone. She felt a lot more relaxed after speaking with Sean. She paged Ron at work. He called her back quickly.

"What is it, honey? Is everything okay?" he asked.

"Yeah, everything is fine. Sean, the manager over at Century 21, called and said how sorry he was about Margaret not informing us about what happened here. He said he would get us a house just as big as this one with lots of land and just as many rooms but in a great safe location. He wants to show us tomorrow, so tell your boss that you want tomorrow off."

"There won't be any demons in the attic or goblins in the basement of these homes will there?"

"Ha, ha. Real funny, Ron. No, he promised me no bad history on any of the houses."

"I will ask my boss and let you know," he said.

"Okay sweetie. Have a good day. I love you."

"I love you too, babe. I have to go."

*****

Michael was in his classroom, and his teacher asked him if his math assignment was done. He handed it to her. She could see something was drawn on the other side of his math assignment, and as she turned the paper over she saw an image that terrified her so much that she dropped the paper. It landed next to Phillip's desk. He picked it up and looked at it with his eyes and mouth wide open. Michael had drawn the Pavor Nocturnus standing over the mutilated body of Andrew Miller. She grabbed it from Phillip and folded it in half so that the rest of the class could not see it.

"Michael, I don't want you drawing this kind of thing ever again," she said assertively.

"Okay, Mrs. Stone. I won't."

At recess, Phillip asked Michael who the monster was eating in the picture.

"A boy named Andrew who was killed by the monster in my house."

"I still think you're bullshitting me."

"You will see on Friday."

"Yeah, okay," said Phillip.

# Chapter 10 The Medallion

After school, Tanya waited in her Honda Accord for Michael. When she saw him, she got out of her car and waved at him. "How was your day, honey?" she asked when he reached the car.

"It was good!"

"Well that is good," she said to him. "Before I drive away, you didn't forget to turn in your math homework did you?"

"No Mom. I turned it in. I promise."

"I believe you, honey," she said to him with a smile.

Ten minutes later, they arrived at Dr. Donahue's office. Michael got out of the car and asked Tanya why he still had to come here.

"Dr. Donahue wants to do some tests," she told him.

"What kind of tests?" he asked.

"I'm not sure yet."

"He's not giving me anymore pills, right Mom?"

"No, he is not."

Dr. Donahue called them both in shortly after they arrived.

"How have you been Michael?" he asked.

"We have both been better," said Tanya as she started to cry. Dr. Donahue handed her a tissue, and Michael gave her a hug.

"I'm sorry to hear that. What's going on?" Dr. Donahue asked.

"Well ever since the move, I have seen some crazy unexplainable things. I don't know what to believe," she said and used the Kleenex to wipe away her tears.

"What kind of things have you been seeing?" asked Dr. Donahue.

"Well at first I wasn't sure if it was stress or the pregnancy. But when I did some research over at my friend Crystal's house it became real."

"Can you be a little more specific?"

Tanya handed Dr. Donahue the article about the three murdered children. She pointed to the pictures of the three kids and said, "I'm seeing the mutilated ghost corpses of Nathan and Brandon."

"I saw Andrew, Nathan, and Brandon," said Michael.

"They were all murdered in the same house I am living in now except for Mike Collins," she said.

"You live in the old Collins home?" asked Dr. Donahue.

"Yes, what do you know about it?" she asked him.

"Well, I am not supposed to share patient information with any of my clients."

"I need you to tell me what you know, for my son's sake," said Tanya.

"Michael Collins was a patient of mine. He was suffering from night terrors that were very similar to the ones your son is suffering from. He claimed that a real monster was after him at night."

"The monster is real," said Michael. "And I met Mike yesterday by Maya's tree, and he told me to paint anything black in my house white. The creature came out of my shelf and attacked me, and it almost got me so I painted it white."

"What do you have to say about all of this, Tanya?" Dr. Donahue asked.

"Despite the fact that I sound like a raving lunatic, I am starting to believe him."

"Why is that? Have you seen evidence of a monster?"

"Well the night Michael said he was attacked by this thing, my husband Ron saw a tall dark figure in Michael's mirror that scared him enough that he took a swing at it with his baseball bat."

"So what was it that he hit?" asked Dr. Donahue.

"Well, he made a good sized hole in Michael's wall."

"But no monster turned up?"

"No, but the next day I couldn't find our cat Tigger anywhere. And he has been missing ever since. I also noticed that the hallway light bulb had been smashed by something and when I went into Mike's room, it smelled like something had died in there. The light bulb on his metal lamp was also broken. And when I checked on top of his dresser, I noticed a stinky slimy dark residue."

"It was slime from the monster coming out of my dresser," Michael exclaimed.

"Well that is strange. What do you think it was, Tanya?"

"At first I thought maybe Michael was playing with his slime on top of the dresser. But then I found it again on my couch the day after Gloria went missing."

"Who is Gloria?"

"Gloria was a lady from a babysitting agency called We Care. My husband hired her because he bought us tickets to a Midsummer Night's Dream."

"An excellent play," said Dr. Donahue with a smile.

"It sure was," said Tanya.

"Okay, go on," he said.

"Well, when we got back, Gloria's car was there, but she wasn't and neither was Michael. He stayed over at my friend Crystal's house because he was so frightened."

"That is scary," he said. "I am sorry you went through all of that, Michael. Did you call the police?"

"Yes, and they questioned me and Michael and my friend Crystal too."

"Did they ever find her?"

"No and her car is still parked outside our house. It is kind of creepy when I look at it," said Tanya.

"What else did you find out?"

"Well our house reeked of that horrible smell when we got home, and the next day I spent a good thirty minutes cleaning the same residue that was on Michael's dresser off of my husband's $2,000 black leather sofa. That same day Michael met Mike Collins."

"That's right. Michael did mention that," said Dr. Donahue. "So Michael, can you tell me why Mike Collins was at the tree yesterday?"

"He was visiting his mom's grave at the big tree in the forest."

"He's not lying. Michael told me that he was an author who lived in Maine with his wife and son, and my Michael showed me his business card that he put on my fridge."

"Wow. He is an author, and he does live in Maine," said Dr. Donahue.

"What kind of author?" asked Tanya.

"He writes horror fiction. He recently wrote a best seller entitled 'The Dark Stalker'. It sold over a million copies the day it went on sale."

"Wow. That is interesting. It must be good."

"I will have to say it is probably the scariest book I have ever read," he said. "But I want to try and stay on subject. Michael, I want to try something a little different with you."

"Like what?" asked Michael.

"Hypnosis," he said.

"Will it hurt me?"

"No, it's harmless."

"Mom, is this safe? I'm a little scared."

"Yes sweetie, it is. And Mommy will be right here with you the whole time."

Michael held onto Tanya's hand.

"Okay, how does it work?" asked Michael

"The technique I am using is called instant induction hypnosis; unlike rapid induction hypnosis which takes anywhere from three to seven minutes, instant induction hypnosis will work within seconds. First, I am going to need you to clear your mind of all thoughts. Think emptiness, and just take in some deep breathes in through the nose and out through the mouth." Michael started to breathe the way Dr. Donahue told him. "Are you feeling relaxed yet, Michael?"

"Yes, I think so."

"Okay, just keep breathing and relax. Pretend you are at the beach and you can hear the sound of the waves crashing down onto the sand." Dr. Donahue gently grabbed Michael's left arm and asked him to look into his eyes. Dr. Donahue stared deeply into Michael's eyes while putting his other hand on Michael's neck. He held it there for seven seconds and then cried out, "Sleep." He moved Michael's head towards him and Michael closed his eyes. "Can you hear me, Michael?"

"Yes."

"How old are you, Michael?"

"I am eight years old."

"Okay, Michael. Did you meet Michael Collins yesterday at his mom's grave behind your house?"

"Yes, I did," he said.

"And what did he say to you?"

"He told me that his mom used to play here when she was a kid and that his dad sprinkled some of her ashes on the tree."

"You mean Robert Collins?"

"Yes."

"Did he say anything else about his dad?"

"He said he built the house for Maya because he loved her very much and also because she loved the tree."

"Anything else about his dad?"

"That he became an alcoholic after his mom Maya died. And that he tried to protect him from the monster but he was blamed for murdering the three kids."

"Do you think Robert murdered the three boys, Michael?"

"No, Pavor Nocturnus did," he said.

"Is that what Mike Collins told you?"

"Yes, but I saw what happened to them in my dream too."

"What happened in your dream?" Michael started to tremble. "Its okay, Michael, you don't have to be afraid here. Can you tell me what happened to the three children in your dream?"

"They were jumping up and down on Mike's bed. And Mike told them to stop and to get off the bed, but they didn't listen. The Pavor Nocturnus came up through the dark sheet on Mike's bed and killed all three of them."

"Oh my god," said Tanya.

"Where was Robert when all of this was happening?" asked Dr. Donahue.

"He was passed out drunk in his bed," said Michael.

"What about Mike Collins? What did he do?"

"He ran and hid in the closet. He turned on a light, and the monster's arm came out of his dad's black jacket and grabbed him by the neck."

"What did he do then? How did he escape?"

"He used the medallion that Maya gave him. He told me it hurt the monster and after that it went away."

"Okay, Michael. Now I want you to tell me what happened the night Gloria went missing."

"I had a bad dream about the monster, and when I woke up and went downstairs the television was on, but Gloria was gone."

"So what did you do?"

"I tried to page my mom, but when I picked up the phone Nathan was on it, and he told me to leave the house now. And after that I heard the Pavor Nocturnus growling upstairs and so I ran for the front door. It was crawling down the stairs so I ran outside and tried to get into Gloria's car, but it was locked."

"So then you went to Crystal's house, right?"

"No, there was a power outage, and the monster grabbed my foot from a black puddle, and it pulled my sock off."

"I found that same sock the next day in a puddle full of that stinky black slime," said Tanya.

"What happened after that, Michael?" asked Dr. Donahue.

"Then I tried to run back into the house but the door was locked so I ran into the forest. That's when I saw a ghost."

"One of the dead children's ghosts?" asked Dr. Donahue.

"No, it was Maya Collins," he said.

"What did she do?"

"She saved my life. She showed me that tree."

"Did you hide in the tree?" asked Dr. Donahue.

"Yes. And I had a dream about Maya when she was a little girl."

"Tell me about it, Michael."

"Well Maya was about my age, and she was swinging on a swing. When she looked up, she saw an angel," he exclaimed.

"What did she do then?"

"She climbed up the tree to where the angel was, but she fell out of it, and the angel caught her."

"Did he say what his name was?"

"Yes, he was the Archangel Michael, and he gave her a medallion. He told her whenever she needed him to say the prayer."

"What prayer?"

"Most powerful of angels protect me from harm," said Michael.

"So you did not stay at Crystal's house that night?"

"No, I stayed in the tree until morning and then I went home."

Dr. Donahue looked at Tanya. "Shit. I am sorry. I lied to you. You're not going to tell the police are you?" she said.

"Well if they ask me about it, since Gloria is now a missing person, by law I have to tell them the truth. But don't worry, I am not going to call them and let them know," he said.

"Thank you, doctor," said Tanya. "So Michael, you said that Mike Collins gave you his business card right?"

"Yes, he sure did," exclaimed Michael.

"Did he give you anything else?" asked Dr. Donahue.

"Yes." Michael reached into his shirt and pulled out the medallion that Mike gave him.

"Oh my god," said Tanya, gazing at it in wonder.

It appeared old with the sun on it, and rays of light were resonating off the sun on the medallion. The names of the four highest Seraphim's in creation were also inscribed into the medallion. The sigil of Michael was written in Aramaic while Enochian runes as old as time itself were in its center.

"That is the Michael Demiurgos medallion. How remarkable," said Dr. Donahue, reaching out to grab it. Suddenly Michael opened his eyes and only the whites of them were showing. He grabbed onto the doctor's wrist fast, and he squeezed onto it so hard that Dr. Donahue screamed out in pain. He tried to pull away with all of his strength, but he could not break from Michael's grasp. Tanya grabbed Michael's arm and said, "Let go, honey. You're hurting him."

He snapped out of it. His eyes returned to normal, and he quickly let go of Dr. Donahue's wrist. He held his wrist in pain and said, "Damn it. I think it is broken."

"I am so sorry," said Tanya. She asked him if there was anything else she could do.

"Please just go," he said.

"Again, I am sorry," she said, leaving the check for him on the table.

She grabbed Michael by his hand and quickly left the office.

"What happened, Mom?" asked Michael.

"Nothing sweetie," she said.

"Why was Dr. Donahue holding his wrist? I didn't do that did I?"

"You don't remember anything that just happened?"

"No, not really."

"Well that is the last time you're getting hypnotized."

"Please Mom. Can you please tell me what happened in there?"

"I think that you might have broken his wrist, sweetie."

"No way. I am sorry, Mom. I didn't know that."

"He shouldn't have tried to grab your medallion," said Tanya.

*Oh no, he knows and my mom does too,* Michael thought to himself. "Mom, I need you to pinky promise me that you won't tell Dad about the medallion."

"Okay, honey, I pinky promise. Can you tell me why?"

"Because I can never take it off. And if Dad finds out about it, he might try and take it away from me."

"Okay, I promise I won't tell him, honey."

"Thanks Mom," he said, giving her a big hug.

"You're welcome, sweetie. That is a beautiful and no doubt special medallion. Always keep it close to your heart, honey."

"I will, Mom. I love you."

"I love you too, my tough little angel."

# Chapter 11 Pavor Nocturnus

"I have some good news, honey," Ron said when he got home.

"You can look at houses with me tomorrow," Tanya replied.

"No, Ralph, Eddie, and Victor are coming over Saturday night to play cards. And I can look at houses with you tomorrow."

She whipped him with a hand towel, and he laughed. "Good. We're going early," she said to him.

"Sounds good to me. I was wondering, babe. Have you heard anything more on Gloria? I saw her car getting towed when I pulled up," said Ron.

"No I haven't, but I sure hope we hear something soon. It's the not knowing that makes this whole thing more terrifying."

"Yeah, but try not to worry or buy into Michael's stories. I'm sure a monster didn't get her."

"But tell me where she could have gone, Ron. Really, I mean it was pouring down rain that night and that black slime I found on the sofa, that's where Michael said she was sitting when they were both watching TV."

"Honestly, I don't know. Maybe she had Alzheimer's and forgot where she was and wandered off into the woods and died, it does happen."

"Maybe you're right. I didn't think about that."

That night she made chicken parmesan for dinner, and Ron and Michael did the dishes. They all went to the TV room afterward. Ron pulled his double bass from its large black case. His father played for years in an orchestra but he died from a heart attack in 1992. He taught Ron how to play "So what" by Miles Davis, and Ron had also learned to play "Scarborough Faire" by Simon and Garfunkel. Michael listened to Ron until Tanya said, "Bedtime, Michael."

"Okay," he said. Tanya gave him a kiss on the cheek.

"Don't I get a kiss too?" asked Ron. She kissed his lips and he started to walk Michael to his bed.

"Can I tuck him in tonight?"

"Sure, babe." He gave Michael a kiss on the head.

"Goodnight, Dad," he said.

"Goodnight, little Tyson."

"You sure got that right," Tanya muttered. As she opened Michael's bedroom door, the smell of paint had faded. She tucked Michael in and gave him a kiss.

"I love you, Mom," he said to Tanya.

"I love you too, sweetie," she said as she left the room.

*****

Michael was awakened by a loud noise. Ron and Tanya were such heavy sleepers that they didn't hear it. A cat meowed outside Michael's door. His heart raced, and it became hard for him to breathe properly as the fear in his chest and stomach grew. He heard a scratch at his door followed by another meow. He pinched himself to make sure he wasn't dreaming. It hurt so he knew he was awake. He put on his glasses and carefully opened the door, grabbing his medallion firmly in his hand. When he looked at his feet, Tigger was not there. And the hallway and bathroom lights were both broken. Frightened, he started to head for his parents' room, but before he got there, he heard the meow again.

"Please let it be Tigger," he said holding the medallion tightly in his hand. As he crept toward the stairs, Pavor Nocturnus poked its head around the corner and hissed at Michael. Within seconds, the monster ran up to him on all fours and grabbed him by the leg, pulling him to the floor. On top of Michael, it opened its mouth full of long sharp fangs and glared at him with its crimson red eyes. As fast as he could speak, Michael said, "Most powerful of angels protect me from harm." He had the medallion pointed right at the monster when suddenly a light force of energy came out of it, knocking the creature through his parents' bedroom door.

Ron jumped up from his bed, grabbing his bat, and told Tanya to dial 911. He ran after it as fast as he could, but it had already scurried down the stairs. Ron flew down the stairs and caught a glimpse of it as it went into the kitchen. It appeared to be a tall man dressed all in black, but it was too dark to make it out, really. He ran into the kitchen and turned on the light, but no one was there.

"I know you're in here, you motherfucker," he said. "Come out, you fucking pussy. I'm right here, you fucking stinky piece of shit." He could smell the thing, but it was nowhere to be found.

"Are you okay, babe?" asked Tanya as she came down the stairs with a Maglite in her hand. Michael was holding onto her leg tightly and rambling on that it was the black monster.

"Did you call the police?" Ron asked her.

"Yes, they're on their way."

"I want you both to go into the bathroom in our room and lock the door right now. It is still in here with us."

"I'm scared, Mommy," said Michael. He shook with fear while squeezing onto her leg so tightly that it was cutting off her circulation.

"Mommy is scared too, honey. Let's go back upstairs." She held his hand and ran back upstairs with him. They went into her bathroom and locked the door. "What in the hell happened?" she asked Michael and he told her what had happened. "I am so sorry," she said.

"Do you believe me now?" he asked her.

"Yes, sweetie. I do." She kissed his head. "I'm scared."

"Me too."

*****

Ron searched the house and was baffled as to why he couldn't find anyone or anything. "There is no way you got out. Everything is dead bolted, and all the windows and doors are locked," he said. He heard a loud knock on the front door and answered it while holding the bat in his hand just in case. He opened the door, and Sheriff Wilson drew his gun.

"Put the bat down," he told Ron.

Ron threw the bat down. "Fucker's still in my house, hiding somewhere."

"I will take it from here," the sheriff said.

"Last I saw he was in the kitchen."

"Don't worry. I will find him."

Ron grabbed the bat then shut and locked the door. Sheriff Wilson searched the house from top to bottom, and the only thing he found was Tanya and Michael locked in the bathroom. She had told Michael to say absolutely nothing to Sheriff Wilson before he got there. Luckily, he did not question them too much as Michael and Tanya both were both too terrified to talk. The Pavor Nocturnus seemed almost as real to Tanya now as it was to Michael. But she knew she would have a hard time convincing Ron.

Sheriff Wilson found the same slimy smelly substance that Tanya found on their black fridge. "This is one sick fuck," he said.

"What did you find?" asked Ron.

"Fecal matter, on your refrigerator," he said.

"That sick motherfucker. Why the hell would someone break into my house, break my bedroom door down, and wipe their shit all over my fridge, then run off without taking anything?"

"Probably because he's a psychopath, but don't worry. I've taken a sample from the fridge and I'll send it to Forensics. We'll catch him with this. Did you get a good look at him?"

"Not really it was too dark to see anything. I think it might have been a tall homeless guy. With really long arms, possibly African American, and dressed completely in black."

"You didn't see his face?"

"No, I just got a glimpse of the back of him. I still think he might be in here. There is no way this guy could have gotten out unless he was like a ninja or something."

"Well, we'll do our best to catch this guy. In the meantime, keep all your doors locked and windows too."

"I assure you they were all locked. I don't know how in the hell he is getting in here."

"Well he must have been pretty damn strong to break down your door like he did. You and your family should be careful. This place does have a bad history."

"What do you know about it?" asked Ron.

"Well my daddy was part of the investigation in the murders of those three young boys back in '76. He said there were all sorts of stories as to what might have happened in this house on that fateful night. Robert's little boy Mike kept going on and on about some monster killing the kids. But I will say it like my daddy said it. Robert Collins is the real monster. If you find anything else, do give me a call," he said handing Ron his business card as he left the house.

"Thanks. Will do," said Ron shutting and locking the door behind him. "I can't fucking believe this," he said as he headed upstairs to check on Tanya and Michael.

"Did he find anything?" asked Tanya.

"No. He did say that this guy is really mental."

"What do you mean mental? Did you see it?" asked Tanya.

"I got a glimpse of him."

"So you know it isn't human, right?"

"No. What I know is this sick twisted fuck was probably here the other night rubbing his feces on our son's dresser because I think it was the same guy I saw in Michael's mirror that night. Tonight he rubbed his shit all over our fridge. Sheriff Wilson took a sample of it. We'll know who this sick fuck is soon."

"Honey, I found black slime in Michael's room, not feces. And I didn't tell you this but I also found it on your leather sofa."

"That motherfucker. I'm going to kill him."

"Well Michael saw it up close and you didn't."

"And it is a monster, right Michael?" said Ron, frustrated.

"He hasn't lied to me once," said Tanya. "I know. It sounded crazy at first. I didn't believe him. But after really listening to what he was trying to tell me, and after what I've seen and heard, it makes more sense," she said.

"Give me some examples Tanya, because you are starting to sound just as irrational as him."

"Well for one, I saw the same two dead kids he saw, and they were trying to warn us to leave this house."

"Can we please go to Crystal's?" asked Michael.

"In a minute, sweetie," Tanya said. "Michael tells me it leaves behind that slime-like residue when it comes into this world from whatever dark place it comes from," she told Ron. "Even Mike Collins warned him about the creature."

"What? That is ridiculous," said Ron. "Why would Mike Collins come all the way here anyway?"

"He was visiting his mom's grave at the tree," Michael exclaimed.

"Mike Collins gave Michael his business card. Michael put it on the fridge yesterday," said Tanya.

"Show me," said Ron.

Tanya, Ron and Michael all walked to the kitchen. Tanya looked at the fridge. "This is the same slime from Michael's room."

"Okay," said Ron. "Where is the card?"

"It's gone, Mom," said Michael.

"Why do you lie for him all the time, Tanya?"

"I'm not fucking lying. I swear to you that I saw him put it there yesterday."

"Okay. Well whoever this fucking psycho is, I think he's still in the house, and it is not safe for you guys here."

"I know. We're going to Crystal's tonight. Come with us, babe."

"I have to catch this guy," said Ron.

"Please, Dad. Come with us. It's dangerous here," said Michael.

"Nothing I can't handle," said Ron. "Don't worry, babe," he said to Tanya. "I'll be by tomorrow to pick you up and look at houses."

"Okay, your choice. But I really wish you would come stay with us tonight," said Tanya.

"Nothing is going to happen to me, babe. I'll be fine."

"Fine, have it your way." Tanya packed a bag for her and Michael and called Crystal. "Can Michael and I stay the night with you tonight?"

"What happened?" Crystal asked.

"Michael was attacked by something, and Ron went after it."

"Oh my god, is everyone okay?"

"Yes, we're okay, but it's not safe here. I would really appreciate it if you'd let me and Michael stay the night."

"Of course. Come on over."

"I owe you big time, girl," said Tanya.

"You don't owe me anything. You know you guys are welcome here anytime. Is Ron okay?"

"He's fine, but he wants to stay at the house. I tried to talk him into coming with us, but he won't listen. You know how hard headed he can be. I'll fill you in on all the details when we get there."

"Okay. See you in a few."

Tanya told Ron to be careful and to come to Crystal's house if he changed his mind.

"I will, babe," he said. "And I promise you, we will get this guy."

She hugged him and started to cry.

"Please don't cry. I'll be fine. Nobody messes with One, Two Ronny Walker's family and gets away with it. I'll see you tomorrow."

*****

Tanya put Michael to bed in Crystal's spare bedroom and filled Crystal in on everything that happened.

"I hope they get whoever or whatever has been terrorizing you guys," Crystal said.

"Ron says that what he saw was human, but Michael swears up and down that it's not."

"So who do you believe?"

"I believe Michael. He already had three close encounters with the thing. And after seeing the mutilated ghosts of those two poor kids and finding out that Robert Collins was innocent. And Tigger went missing the same night Michael claimed he first saw the thing. There's also that nasty dark residue I've been finding on our black furniture. It all started making more sense to me."

"What started making sense?"

"That something dark and sinister is after my family."

"I'll always be here for you," Crystal told her.

"You're like my sister and my best friend. I can't thank you enough for all you've done for my family and me. From the bottom of my heart, thank you, Crystal."

"You're welcome. I can only imagine how much stress you've been under. How have you been feeling health wise?"

"Well when I stress I get a kick from baby sometimes. I really worry about my baby going through this with me."

"It's a good thing you guys are looking at new houses tomorrow then."

"Yeah, the sooner we can be out of this nightmare the better. Let me take you shopping tomorrow. I really could use a break from this fucking nightmare I have been living."

"Aren't you and Ron looking at houses tomorrow?"

"That is actually today," said Tanya looking down at her watch.

"Oh shit, it's nearly 3 a.m.," said Crystal as she looked at the clock on the wall. "We better get to bed."

"Good idea," said Tanya.

"I would love to go shopping with you tomorrow. I could do with some new perfume."

"Great. It will be fun."

"Goodnight, girl." Tanya gave Crystal a hug. They went into the guest bedroom where Michael was fast asleep.

"I promise this nightmare will be over soon," Tanya whispered to Michael.

*****

Ron searched the house again. He even searched outside, but he found nothing. He looked at the busted bedroom door and thought, *who could do that with one punch or kick? Whoever it was must have charged at the door full speed, like an angry linebacker on PCP.* He cleaned up the wreckage and took measurements then sat on his bed with his baseball bat next to him. His heart raced fast as the anxiety grew from not knowing. "What in god's name could have done that to our door? That didn't sound like no human to me. Maybe I'm just losing my fucking mind like everyone else around here," he said aloud. He breathed heavily. Unable to relax he went downstairs and opened a bottle of whiskey. He downed half a glass and went back upstairs to grab a Valium from the medicine cabinet. As soon as he turned on the light, he saw a dead boy missing his lower jaw and both of his arms. Half of his neck was missing, and he had huge lacerations running down his face. He screamed and dropped his glass of whiskey as he spun around to face the kid. There was no kid. He looked into the mirror again, but it was only his reflection. "Fuck this place," he said. He took a Valium and picked up the broken pieces of glass. As he put the last piece of glass into the trash, he stood. There in the mirror was the same dead kid, Nathan, missing both of his eyes. It was the same boy Michael and Tanya saw. "What the fuck?" Ron yelled.

"The monster's real," said Nathan. He grabbed his bat and went to go back into the bathroom but stopped when he heard what sounded like a cat meowing. He followed the noise, and it led him to a cupboard. He grabbed the cupboard door with one hand with his baseball bat in the other. As soon as he opened it, Tigger came flying out, hissing and meowing.

"Fuck, Tigger. You scared the shit out of me." He grabbed Tigger and started petting him. "Were you in that cupboard this whole time?" Tigger purred as Ron stroked him. "It's good to see you too, boy," he said lying down with him in his bed.

# Chapter 12 House Hunting

The next morning Ron's pager woke him. Not a minute later, the house phone rang and he staggered down the stairs and answered it.

"What the hell are you doing?" It was Tanya. "We're supposed to be looking at houses with Sean."

"I'm sorry, babe. I'm on my way now. Love you. Bye," he said hanging up the phone. He got ready and drove to Crystal's as quickly as he could. He was still fairly tired from taking the Valium and drinking the whiskey last night, and thoughts of the two dead children he had seen in the mirror haunted him. He took in a few deep breaths to calm himself. He knew Tanya might still be mad at him. Once he arrived, he saw Michael standing with Tanya and Crystal and another man. The man introduced himself as Sean and apologized to Ron for Margaret's mistake.

"Do you know just how haunted that place is?" Ron asked.

"Your wife has told me plenty," he said with a smile.

"Yeah, well let me tell you now. Last night after some psychopath broke into our house and rubbed his feces all over the front of our fridge, he took off, and two ghosts visited me. One was missing his eyes, and the other one was so badly mangled it looked like he had been put arms and face first right into a wood chipper."

"You saw Andrew and Nathan, Daddy?" asked Michael.

"Yes, Daddy met Andrew and Nathan last night, slugger," said Ron.

"I told you they were real," said Michael.

"And I am sorry for doubting you both," said Ron.

"My god that is terrible," said Sean, "but you won't have to worry for long because I am going to show you two beautiful new houses as nice and as big as the one you are in now."

"I swear to you if any of these places have any bad history or ghosts living in them, I will personally hold you responsible. You don't want that, trust me," said Ron.

"I understand," said Sean, "and I promise you no bad history."

The first house they saw had four bedrooms and two bathrooms with a decent size backyard and a two car garage. Ron and Michael liked it but the kitchen was too small for Tanya.

The next house had a nice driveway. Sean showed them the garage first. "Wow, look at the size of this garage. Both our cars could fit in here with no problem," said Ron as he opened the white cupboards. "We could store everything we own in here and then some," he said with a smile.

The inside of the house was huge with a large dining area with cathedral ceilings. "Oh my god, honey. The kitchen has an island," said Tanya.

"You could do all of your cooking here and have plenty of counter space." said Ron.

Sean led them upstairs to the master bedroom as Michael explored.

"I can't believe it. Look at this Jacuzzi tub, Ron."

"Nice. I could definitely get used to that," said Ron as he wrapped his arms around Tanya gently kissed her neck.

"Mom, come and see the bedrooms. They are amazing," said Michael as he grabbed Tanya's hand and led her to one of the bedrooms.

"Wow, these rooms are big."

"Can we move in today, Mom? Please, can we?" asked Michael.

"No sweetie, we can't today."

"Are you guys ready to see the best part?" Sean asked.

"Yeah, sure," they all said.

Sean led them into the backyard.

"Look at that pool and spa," said Ron as he stared in amazement.

"That's nearly half the size of an Olympic pool," said Tanya.

"That water is calling to me," said Ron.

"That's awesome," said Michael as he rushed to the diving board and started bouncing on it. "Can we get it?"

"This house is really just $200,000?" asked Ron.

"Well technically speaking, no. But I was able to pull some strings, and I can give you the same deal that you got on your first house."

"And no bad history?" asked Ron.

"No bad history," said Sean.

"You have just made us one happy family, Sean. I apologize for what I said earlier," said Ron.

"Don't worry. It was totally understandable. And again, I am sorry for what you and your family have been suffering through and for Margaret not telling you about the murders."

"It's not your fault, Sean. In fact if it wasn't for you, none of this would be possible," said Ron. "So thank you." Ron looked him in the eye and shook his hand.

"It has been my pleasure," Sean said with a smile.

"So when can we move in?" asked Ron.

"I could probably close escrow as soon as Monday," said Sean.

"How does that sound, babe?" he asked Tanya.

"It sounds great. Michael seems to love it too. Thanks again, Sean," said Tanya. "This place is absolutely wonderful."

"It really has been my pleasure," said Sean with a smile. "And please feel free to page me if you have any concerns or questions that need answering. I wish you many years of happiness, peace, and joy in your lovely new home," he said. He got into his Mercedes and left waving goodbye to them.

"What a sweet guy," said Tanya.

"Yeah he was, wasn't he?" said Ron. "Oh yeah. I've got another surprise for you both."

"Oh yeah, what is it?" asked Tanya.

"Yeah, Dad, what is it?"

"Well now, it wouldn't be a surprise if I told you now would it?" Tanya and Michael followed him home, both of them wondering what the surprise could be. When they arrived back home Ron made them both close their eyes. Tanya held Michael's hand and Ron held onto Tanya's hand. He opened the door with his key and led them both inside. The house smelled as if something had died in it.

"It smells terrible in here. You're not going to show us a dead body, are you?" she asked.

"Okay, you can open your eyes now."

They both opened their eyes and lying on the floor was Tigger, alive and well.

"It's Tigger," yelled Michael picking him up and petting him.

"Does that look like a dead body to you?" asked Ron.

"Where did you find him?" asked Tanya.

"He was inside the white cupboard upstairs," said Ron.

"He was hiding in there this whole time?" asked Tanya.

"Apparently so," said Ron.

"He was hiding from the monster," said Michael.

"Did you see it?" asked Tanya.

Ron took her upstairs and explained everything he had seen. Did their ghosts say anything to you?" asked Tanya. Ron turned silent and put his head down. "Honey, did any of their ghosts speak to you?" she asked him again.

"Uh, yeah, the one missing his eyes did."

"What did he say?" she asked him, but he chose to ignore her. "What did Nathan say, Ron?" she said louder.

"He said that the monster is real, okay?"

"So you believe Michael now, right?" she asked him. He continued to ignore her. "Please tell me you believe our son now, Ron," she said frustrated.

"I don't know what the hell I believe," he said. "I'm going out."

"You can't keep running away from this, Ron."

"I'm not running away. I have to get a few things."

"Like what?"

"You'll see. I'll be back in an hour," he said and left.

"Mommy, it stinks in here," said Michael. She was starting to feel nauseous from the smell.

"I know, baby," said Tanya. It seemed really bad in the TV room. She grabbed her fly swatter and started killing flies on Ron's black leather sofa. There was no more of that stinky slime in the room or the house, but it wouldn't be the first time Tigger had brought a dead animal into the house. She lit some incense, put it on the table by the couch, and lit candles throughout the house. She waited anxiously for Ron to return home.

# Chapter 13 Security Cameras

A few hours later Ron came back with a brand new bedroom door as well as three top-of-the-line security cameras and a monitor where he could see and hear what was going on at all times from his room. "If this bastard decides to come back tonight, I will catch him on this," he said to Tanya.

"That's great, babe," she said to him smiling.

"I'm going to put one downstairs in the den facing the kitchen entrance and stairs too. I'm also going to put one overlooking the living room where the television is. And the third one I am going to put in the hallway outside the baby's room so we can see Michael's bedroom and our bedroom at all times."

"I am so glad you bought these cameras, babe. Don't you think we should put one in Michael's room too?"

"Don't worry. I bought Michael a new lock for his bedroom door, and we'll see anyone who tries to get in. I also bought these locks for the windows."

"You're the best," she said and hugged him.

"I just want to protect my family."

He spent the rest of his day off installing the cameras and setting up the monitor. He put in a new, sturdier bedroom door with a decent lock and replaced Michael's door handle with one that had a lock and required a key to open. Ron put the key onto his keychain. He put new locks on all the windows in the house and told Tanya to stand downstairs in front of the kitchen entrance. He had Michael stand in the hallway upstairs.

"Wow these work great," he said. "I can see you from my bedroom, slugger."

"Let me see, Dad." Michael ran into the bedroom.

"Look, there's Mommy on camera one." Ron pointed to Tanya on his monitor.

"I see you, Mommy," Michael screamed.

"You do?" she said.

"Yes, and I can hear you too," he yelled.

"Now I want you to go sit on my leather sofa."

"Okay, Dad," said Michael, running downstairs and sitting on the sofa. "Can you see me?" he screamed.

"Yes, I can, and I can hear you just fine too. Send Mommy up now," he said loud enough for Tanya to hear.

"Dad wants you, Mom," he yelled.

"I know, sweetie. I heard him."

When she got into the room, she saw Michael on the monitor.

"Can you see me, Mom?" Michael asked loudly.

"I sure can. You don't have to yell. I can hear you just fine."

"Michael, I want you to go into the kitchen now and then come upstairs and stand in the middle of the hallway. Can you do that for me?" yelled Ron.

"Yes, Dad." Michael proceeded to walk into the kitchen. Ron saw him enter the kitchen and look in the fridge. He could also see Michael as he walked upstairs and when he stood in the hallway.

"This thing is incredible," Tanya exclaimed.

"Isn't it great?" said Ron.

They all felt more at ease that night. Michael slept in his own bed and because he was a bit frightened, he still had Tigger with him and that made him feel better. He was also able to relax a bit more knowing his mom and dad were watching the hallway. He hung a king-sized white sheet on his ceiling to cover the crawl space and his closet mirror and fastened it to the ceiling with thumbtacks. He slept with the light on.

Ron spent a good hour watching the cameras and then turned over and fell asleep. Early the next morning, he checked the surveillance tape before work. He fast-forwarded through most of it. There was no activity. "What is that smell?" said Ron. He checked on Michael before he left and found him and Tigger fast asleep in bed. He kissed him on the head and left for work.

Tanya got Michael up for school and made him scrambled eggs. He ate them up fast and grabbed his bag from the hook in the kitchen. He gave his mom a hug and hurried out the door to the bus stop.

Tanya was glad to see him in a happier mood. She took a shower and got ready. It still smelled horrible inside the house. "Damn it, Tigger. What in the hell did you bring in here?" She sprayed the TV room with Lysol and burned some incense. She killed some more flies that were hovering about mainly in the TV room then she searched everywhere for the dead animal, but she found nothing. She called Crystal and asked her what time she wanted to go shopping.

"What time is it now?" asked Crystal.

"Almost 9:30."

"Are you dressed?"

"Yeah, I'm ready."

"Well, come on over girl," said Crystal.

"Okay, see you in ten." Tanya grabbed her purse and keys.

# Chapter 14 Shopping and Shooting

Tanya and Crystal took Crystal's black Dodge Ram truck to the mall. They went to Nordstrom and Tanya bought Crystal a brand new Chanel perfume she fell in love with called Allure. Tanya liked it so much she bought a bottle of it for herself as well. It smelled of vanilla and flowers with hints of spice.

"Ron is going to like this," said Tanya.

"I think Sean will like it too," said Crystal.

"You have a new man? When did this happen?"

Crystal smiled and rolled her eyes over and down. "You two have already met."

"Oh my god, Sean our realtor?" she asked with a big smile.

"Yeah, he gave me his card that day and said if I was in need of a new house or a nice dinner to give him a call. So I called him and he is taking me out to dinner Friday night."

"He was really sweet and really cute."

"Yeah I know right? There is something I really like about him."

"Well I really hope it works out for you two. You would make a really cute couple."

"Thank you. Me too."

After they finished at Nordstrom, they went into a shop called Mystique. They sold crystals, fantasy figurines, and incense as well as spell books and alchemical ingredients.

"I love this store," said Crystal grabbing some sage.

"What do you do with that?"

"Well, you light it and wave it around your house, and it clears away any negative energies or bad spirits that may be troubling you. I would strongly suggest that you burn a bundle as soon as you get home, honey."

"That sounds like a wonderful idea." Tanya grabbed a few bundles for herself.

"I'll get it for us," said Crystal.

"Are you sure? You don't have to, sweetie."

"But I want to. Especially after everything you've told me. You're going to need it, honey."

"I don't know what I would do without you."

Tanya grabbed many different types of incense sticks and burners.

"What's with all the incense, girl? Are you planning on opening up your own booth at the Ren Faire?" asked Crystal.

"No, Tigger killed something outside and hid it somewhere in the damn house. It smells horrible and I can't find the dead animal anywhere."

"That's great you found Tigger. Where was he?"

"Ron found him hiding in the cupboard the night I stayed at your house."

"Was he in there this whole time?"

"Yes. He scared the shit out of my husband when he found him."

"That's pretty strange," said Crystal.

"Tell me about it. There are some beautiful crystals in here, Crystal," said Tanya. "I love that name," she said with a smile.

"You know, before I was born my mom was a very spiritual woman. She would collect all sorts of crystals, and she would tell me that when everyone got together for the holidays it was always fun and cheery. They would all laugh and tell jokes and have a great time. One Christmas when everyone was at the dinner table, she announced that she was pregnant and every single crystal in the house started to resonate as if they were singing in celebration. That's when my mom realized she was going to have a baby girl and name her Crystal."

"That is one of the most beautiful stories I have ever heard," said Tanya. Just then, she spotted one of the most clear and beautiful crystals she had ever seen.

Large and flawless, it sparkled and glistened more than any crystal she had seen before. "I have to get this crystal," she said aloud.

"Wow, that is absolutely gorgeous," said Crystal.

"Every time I look at it, I will think of you and that wonderful story you just told me."

"It's all true."

"That is pretty magical," said Tanya.

"I thought so too." Crystal gave Tanya a big hug.

"You know you are my best friend in the whole world too," said Crystal to Tanya.

"I absolutely do."

Tanya paid for the crystal and incense and asked the cashier if she could come back and get the crystal after they finished shopping as it was pretty heavy.

"No problem at all. I will keep it safe here for you," said the cashier.

"Thank you so much."

Crystal paid for the sage and put most of it into Tanya's bag. "Thanks, Crystal, for getting me the sage," said Tanya.

"Anytime, sweetie."

They looked in a few more shops then Tanya spotted Mike Collins's novel just inside a bookstore on a large rack. It said "The Dark Stalker - #1 bestseller" on the rack. Tanya picked up the book. On the cover was the scariest looking monster she had ever seen. It looked exactly as her son described.

"Oh my god. That is scary," said Crystal staring at the monster on the cover. "What book is that?"

"This is the monster Michael has been seeing at night," she told Crystal.

"You have got to be fucking kidding me. Please tell me you are joking."

Tanya broke out in tears. She cried aloud as she slammed the book to the ground "This fucker is after my son." One of the employees asked Tanya if she was all right. "You know what?" She picked up the book from the floor, stormed over to the cashier, and told him she wanted to buy the book.

"Tanya, you don't have to get this," said Crystal.

"No. I do have to get this, Crystal. This is the only way I will know the truth." She paid for the book and went back to pick up her crystal and incense from Mystique. Once they got into Crystal's truck, she broke out in tears as she stared at the monster on the book.

"What in the world could this demon possibly want from my son?" said Tanya.

"I can't imagine what you are going through. But you and your family are all welcome to stay at my house until the move," said Crystal.

"I'm sorry I yelled at you in the bookstore."

"It's okay, sweetie. If that thing was after my family, or me I would be terrified and angry too. If this thing is indeed real, is there any way to stop it?"

"Michael said he used his medallion to hurt the monster the other night when it attacked him."

"That thing is so fucking scary, Tanya. I hope you never have to see it for real."

"I just wish Michael never did. Ron spent a few thousand dollars on some security cameras that he set up in the house. If this thing is indeed real, we will see it on the monitor."

"Does Ron own a gun?"

"No, but he is a hell of a fighter."

"After what it did to those kids, I'm pretty sure fists won't do it," said Crystal. "You don't have any weapons?"

"Ron has an aluminum baseball bat."

"I don't think that is enough either." Crystal started the truck and headed back to her house. "I've got something for you, but I will need it back once you move into your new house."

"What is it?"

"I'll show you when we get there."

Ten minutes later, they arrived at Crystal's house.

"Okay, what is it?" asked Tanya.

"Come here," said Crystal as she led Tanya into her bedroom. She grabbed a wooden box from her drawer and opened it. Inside was a nickel-plated .38 special with rosewood grips and a box of ammo.

"Where did you get this?" asked Tanya.

"Tony gave it to me before he got locked up."

"Well I don't want to get in trouble for having someone else's gun."

"Don't worry. It's untraceable."

"I still have a few hours before Michael gets out of school. Can you show me how this thing works?"

"Sure. But let's take your car so you can drop me off afterwards and then get Michael."

"Good idea."

The two of them got into the car, and Crystal gave Tanya directions to the indoor shooting range. Tanya paid for them both to shoot and Crystal purchased extra ammo along with a couple of targets. The range master provided them with free eye and ear protection. They were assigned to lane two and Crystal loaded the .38 with ammo and explained to Tanya how to stand and how to hold the gun properly. She told her to cock the lever, take a deep breath in, and squeeze the trigger as she exhaled. Tanya did exactly as she said and hit the target in the center of his head.

"Great shot," said Crystal. "Let's see you do it again." She sent the target out fifteen feet. Tanya repeated what she did before. She took in a deep breath, and as she breathed out, she gently squeezed the trigger. When Crystal reeled in the target, they saw that the second round was only about an inch to the right of where the first round hit. "Wow, very impressive," said Crystal.

"This is fun," said Tanya.

"Now I want you to aim for his heart, Tanya." Crystal put the target out about twenty feet this time. Tanya took aim and breathed in deeply once again, squeezed the trigger, and hit the mark. "Okay, now empty the chamber into his head."

Tanya took in a deep breath and fired the last two rounds directly into the target's head and squeezed the trigger again but she spent all five rounds.

"Wow girl, that is rare," said Crystal.

"What is rare?"

"When you squeezed the trigger just then your hands were completely still."

"Well I ran out of ammo."

"Yeah, but most people jerk the gun upward once they fire that last round and go to fire it again," said Crystal, reeling in the target.

"So that is a good thing, right?"

"Girl, you're a natural. You just hit every part of him that I asked you to, and right on the mark with excellent grouping too."

"Thank you, Crystal. That was so much fun. Let's see what you got, girl."

Crystal emptied the spent shell casings from the chamber and quickly loaded five new live rounds into the gun. She put the target out twenty feet and took aim then fired one round after the next bang, bang, bang, bang, bang. She reeled in the target. She had shot out both of the target's eyes and hit his nose, heart, and crotch as well.

"Wow that was amazing. I'm surprised you're not a cop."

"Yeah, I wouldn't qualify. I've done too many drugs in the past."

They shot the entire box of ammo and half of a new box. Tanya dropped Crystal off at her house. "Thank you, Crystal. I had a wonderful day. Thanks for the gun, sage and shooting lesson. I hope your date goes well with Sean this Friday," said Tanya.

"Thank you, girl. I had a blast. And thank you so much for the amazing perfume. I think Sean is going to love it."

"Yeah, I think Ron will too. See you this Saturday."

Tanya drove home, and as soon as she opened the door, Tigger ran outside, startling her. "Damn it, Tigger," she said. She went inside. "Damn it stinks in here. Now I know why you were in such a hurry to get out, boy," she said aloud. She lit two incense sticks and put them both in holders she had just bought. She set them both on the table in the TV room and lit another one she set on the dining room table. Surprised by how many more flies there were in the house, she went on a fly swatting spree. When she finished, she cleaned up their corpses with a brush and dustpan. She put the big crystal she had just bought upstairs on her bedside table. It looked beautiful. It was ever so clear and sparkly. She absolutely loved it. She remembered the sage Crystal had bought her, lit a bundle, and smoked the entire house, starting with her room then Michael's room. After that, she smoked the upstairs hallway and the rest of the rooms upstairs. She headed downstairs and smoked the rest of the house. She grabbed her new book and sat down on the couch and got comfy. The more of the book she read, the more she believed Michael was telling the truth. The book was absolutely terrifying, and the way Mike Collins described the monster in the book was almost the same as her son described it in real life.

# Chapter 15 "What a Stink"

Tanya had just finished chapter five of "The Dark Stalker" when she heard a loud knock at the door. Startled, she jumped up from her chair. Her heart raced as she opened the door. It was Michael holding Tigger in his arms.

"Hi, sweetie. You scared Mommy."

"I'm sorry, Mom." Michael set Tigger down on the floor. "It really stinks in here. Did something die?"

"Yeah, Tigger must have killed an animal outside and brought it in. He hid it really good. I've looked everywhere and can't find it."

"Can I go outside and play?"

"Homework first. You know the rules."

"Fine." Michael went upstairs with his backpack.

Tanya read more of her book, and chapter after chapter it became scarier and scarier. About an hour later, Michael came downstairs and asked if he could go outside now. "Are you done with all of your homework?" she asked.

"Yes, I'm all done."

"Okay, put your math homework in your math book between the pages you did and then put your science homework in your science book between the same pages you did it on."

"I didn't have science homework today."

"Well then put whatever homework you did complete in the same book you did it from, between the pages that you worked on. Then put them in your backpack and bring it down for me to look at."

Michael ran upstairs and did as his mom told him. Tanya earmarked the page in her book where she had stopped reading. She put a cushion over it so Michael could not see it. Minutes later, he came back down and gave Tanya his backpack. She opened it up and looked over his homework.

"Good job, sweetie," she said.

"Can I go out and play now?" he asked.

"Yes, you may. But stay close and check back with me in a couple of hours."

"Okay," said Michael and ran outside to play.

Tanya continued her reading. Two hours passed, and Michael came home. Tanya decided it was time to put up the book. Just reading about the monster terrified her. She couldn't begin to imagine just how terrified Michael must have been when he actually saw it the first time and when it attacked him. Part of her still thought it could be some sick twisted psycho of a man, but sooner or later the cameras would reveal the truth. She hid the book in her dresser drawer so Michael wouldn't find it then stared at the beautiful crystal she had just bought. It truly was a sight to behold, flawless in its beauty.

A few minutes later, Tanya heard Ron's truck pull into the driveway, and she came downstairs. As Ron entered the house, he waved his hand over his nose and yelled, "Whoa what a stink. It smells like a can of sour, rotten, assholes in here!"

"Thank you for that image," said Tanya sarcastically then lit more incense as Ron tried to find out where the smell was coming from.

"It is definitely in the TV room," he said, but he could not find whatever was creating the rancid smell.

"Honey how does Fettuccine Alfredo sound for dinner"

"Sounds great as long as I don't have to smell this as I am eating it," said Ron.

Ron brought some cardboard boxes from his truck into the garage, as well as a tape gun to use for the move. Underneath the boxes was a brand new BMX bike for Michael's ninth birthday. He carefully lifted it out of the truck and placed it strategically in the garage behind his old ping-pong table, hidden completely out of sight then went back inside.

"Tanya, I'd rather eat with my nose up my ass than eat in this house with that stink," he said.

"That's disgusting, Ron," she said.

"It's no more disgusting than that god awful smell that is about to make me puke. Honey, let's eat outside tonight."

"It's starting to get cold, and it might rain tonight."

"Well, I'm not eating in the house with that smell. Period."

"Then you can set up the dinner plates and silverware at the outside table."

"No problem. Michael, come down here and lend me a hand," he yelled from the bottom of the stairs.

"Okay, Dad. I'm coming," said Michael running fast down the stairs. "What do you need help with?"

"I need you to help me set the table outside for dinner."

Michael grabbed some silverware from the kitchen drawer. Ron grabbed the plates and glasses. They both set the outside dinner table. "Hey, slugger, can you also grab me some matches and a few of those good smelling candles your mom keeps inside?"

"Sure thing, Dad," said Michael.

"That a boy."

Soon Ron and Michael had the outside table set and the candles lit. Tanya spritzed herself with the Allure perfume she had bought at the mall and served them both their dinner.

"Wow, this is some amazing fettuccine," said Ron.

"It sure is. Thanks Mom," said Michael.

"You're welcome, boys," she said. "This was a good idea. It does smell pretty disgusting inside."

"Yeah, no kidding. This is kind of nice for a change," said Ron.

"I wish it could be like this all the time but without us being haunted and tormented." Tanya teared up and the baby kicked inside her. "Come here quick boys. The baby just kicked."

They both rushed to her and put their hands on her stomach. It kicked again.

"Wow, I felt that," said Ron.

"I did too," said Michael.

Ron gave Tanya a hug and kiss and said, "I love you so much, baby."

"I love you too," said Tanya.

"I love that perfume you're wearing. What is it?"

"It's a new one called Allure by Chanel. Crystal and I both got a bottle of it today."

"What? You two went shopping today?"

"Yeah, I bought a beautiful crystal that I put on my nightstand and some more incense too."

"Well I really like that perfume, but I don't think you can buy enough incense to make that rotten smell go away. But don't you worry about the house. We'll be in a new and improved one next week, free of ghouls and ghosts and bad smells."

"Thanks, babe." Tanya gave them both kisses. "Which reminds me, I need to light some more incense." She headed back inside.

"Come on, slugger. Let's clean this mess up for your mom," said Ron.

"Okay," said Michael, grabbing the plates with all the silverware on top of them.

Ron grabbed the glasses and candles from the table and opened the door for Michael. They brought them inside and Tigger followed them into the house.

"Do you mind doing dishes while I relax for a bit upstairs?" asked Tanya.

"No, we don't mind, right, slugger?"

"No, not at all," said Michael.

"You two are the best," said Tanya.

After Ron and Michael finished washing the dishes, they sat down and watched some television together. Tigger joined them. Even over the incense, they could smell something rotting inside the house. Ron looked at Tigger.

"I'm going to keep you inside permanently if you bring just one more dead thing into the house, boy. You got that?"

"It smells really bad, Dad," said Michael.

"I'd rather smell a dirty litter box all day for the rest of my life than suffer through this smell for three more days. God help us," said Ron.

"We will for sure need his help if the monster comes back," said Michael.

"If any monster comes here your dad will take care of it, slugger. Don't you worry."

They watched some cartoons for a bit, and Tanya came downstairs.

"It's bedtime, Michael. Come on. I'll tuck you in," she said.

Ron said, "Goodnight, son. I love you."

"Goodnight, Dad. I love you too."

Tanya took Michael upstairs. Tigger followed and jumped into bed with Michael. Tanya tucked him in and gave him a kiss. "Goodnight, sweetie," she said. As she turned to leave, Michael said, "Mom."

"Yeah, sweetie, what is it?"

"The other night when I used my medallion on the monster, I think I hurt it."

"Well that's good, isn't it?"

"Yeah, I guess so, but do you think it will come back for me?"

"No, baby, I don't think so."

"But what if it does?"

"Then we will see it on the camera and your dad will kill it."

"What if it kills dad though?"

"Don't worry. It won't," said Tanya. "And after what I saw you do to Dr. Donahue, I don't think it will want to mess with you either."

"I love you, Mom."

"I love you too, sweetie," said Tanya, shutting the door. She went into her room, grabbed her book from her drawer, and started to read.

# Chapter 16 "One Scary Book"

Meanwhile Ron was going over the surveillance tape from the night before; nothing unusual or out of the norm, so he headed upstairs. He opened his new bedroom door, and Tanya screamed and jumped out of the bed.

"Whoa, relax babe. It's just me," he said to her.

"I'm sorry, babe. This book I'm reading is pretty scary," said Tanya.

"I guess so. Let me see?"

Tanya handed him the book, and as he looked at the cover, he had a flashback from the night he saw the dark figure run into the kitchen. He threw the book down. "What is it, babe? Are you okay?"

"Yeah, that is one scary monster."

"Tell me about it. I can only imagine how Michael feels."

"What do you mean?"

"Mike Collins wrote this book about the monster our son has been seeing," she said. The mere thought sent shivers up and down Ron's spine.

"Oh enough of this shit already, Tanya. Why in the hell would you read something so terrifying before bedtime anyway?"

"To know the truth."

"The truth about what?"

"That this monster is just as real as you and me."

"Oh, bullshit."

"When will you start to believe us? When it bites you in the ass?"

"I believe in what I can see, and so far I haven't seen evidence of any monster."

"What about Andrew and Nathan and how they looked? I mean what kind of human being could to something like that to a child? He even told you the monster was fucking real, Ron. What more do you need to believe?"

"Well, if it is real, I will see it on the monitor, and then I will believe. But for now, I want you to stop reading this bullshit." Ron chucked the book into the bedside trashcan.

"You can be a real asshole sometimes. You know that?"

"Yeah, well, I am just looking out for you, baby," he said walking into the bathroom.

He brushed his teeth while Tanya grabbed the book from out of the trashcan and put it back into her dresser drawer. She lay down and fell asleep minutes later. Ron set up a brand new tape and hit record then lay down next to her and fell asleep shortly after.

Later that night, Tanya felt Ron rubbing her belly and turned to face him. As she opened her eyes, all that was left of Ron was his head, connected to his spine, connected to his lower torso. The rest of him was scattered about the room. Blood was everywhere. His rib cage and intestines hung from the ceiling fan, and the Pavor Nocturnus was using the hand on Ron's severed arm to rub her belly. Tanya was paralyzed with fear. She could not scream. She could not move at all, but she could hear, and she could see as the demon tossed Ron's arm to the ground and used its long sharp index finger to cut open her belly.

"No, not my baby," yelled Tanya, imagining that this demon was going to eat her child in front of her.

She woke up screaming and woke Ron. She looked down at her belly crying. "What happened?" asked Ron.

"The monster he killed you and tried to take our baby," said Tanya crying and holding Ron tightly.

"Don't worry, babe. I'm here. It was just a nightmare."

Michael knocked on the door. "Mom, are you okay?" he yelled.

"Yeah, Mom is okay. She just had a bad dream. Go back to bed slugger," Ron answered.

"Okay, Dad," said Michael heading back to bed.

Ron finally calmed her down a bit. "I told you that you shouldn't watch or read horror before bedtime," he told Tanya.

"It seemed so real. I actually felt your hand rubbing my belly," she said.

"It was just a bad dream, babe, nothing more."

The next day he was up before Tanya and decided to check the tape. He saw Michael come out of his room and knock on their door and he heard him say, "Mom, are you okay?" He even heard himself tell Michael to go back to bed and watched Michael go back into his room. "Now that is impressive," he said aloud. A few minutes later, the hallway light flickered off then on again. He fast forwarded through the rest of the tape but noticed nothing else unusual, so he dressed and left for work.

Later Tanya woke and got Michael ready for school. As he grabbed his bag from the hook in the kitchen, she told him, "Have a good day in school, sweetie."

"What happened last night, Mom?" asked Michael.

"Mommy just had a bad dream. That's all."

"Was it about the monster?"

"No, I just read something scary, and I had a silly nightmare about it. That's all, honey."

"Oh. Well I had a dream about the monster," said Michael.

"What happened?"

"He was trying to reach for me through the hole Dad made in the wall, but he couldn't get me."

"Good, baby. I'm glad you were all right." She gave him a hug and a kiss. "You know you are my brave boy, and I love you very much."

"Thanks, Mom. I love you too."

"Don't forget to turn in your homework."

"Don't worry. I won't," he said as he headed out the door to the bus.

Tanya began thinking about what could have happened to Gloria. Even though Ron's story made some sense to her, she couldn't help but think that the Dark

Stalker got her. It still smelled bad inside the house so she lit some more incense and decided to do some laundry. As she gathered the dirty clothes from Michael's room, she noticed four lacerations in the poster that she had hung over the hole in the wall. It looked as if Freddy Krueger had a go at it. She took it down and noticed more of the same smelly black residue inside the wall that she had been finding on the furniture.

"Oh my god, what if Michael is right? What on earth could this thing be? What does it want from my son?" she said to herself.

She cleaned it up and grabbed some spackle and the can of white paint Michael had used to paint his dresser and repaired the wall. She went to the grocery store to pick up some groceries and a birthday cake for Michael then put the paint and spackle back in the garage. She proceeded to put everything black that she owned and everything black that Ron owned into large trash bags and boxes just like Michael had done days before. She had read in her book that this creature came from a dark world and that the only way it could come into this one is through black objects just as Michael had said to her before she read the book. The whole idea of a monster sounded like nothing more than a dreamed up nightmare but one that felt increasingly real with each passing day. She packed up anything and everything black she could lift into the cardboard boxes that Ron had brought home and used the tape gun to seal them shut. Afterward she sprayed Lysol throughout the TV room and lit more incense. She opened all the windows to air it out.

"Tigger, I'm never going to forgive you for this," she said. She went upstairs and grabbed her book that felt like more of a survival guide. And as terrifying as it was, she couldn't stop reading it, wondering what clues she might find next. It told a lot about Mike and how the creature ate his dog and also how he used his medallion to hurt the monster A few hours later, the phone rang and startled her. She jumped out of bed and hurried to answer it.

"Hello?"

"Yes, this is Sheriff Wilson. Is Ron or Tanya Walker in?" came a voice from the other end of the line.

"Yes, this is Tanya. How may I help you?"

"Yes, I wanted to let you know that results of the tests from the sample I took from your fridge the other night came back from forensics."

"So you caught the guy?"

"No ma'am. Forensics said they have never seen anything like it before."

"So it wasn't shit?"

"No ma'am. It wasn't. In fact, it is of unknown origin."

"Unknown origin . . . What is that supposed to mean?"

"It means they don't know what it is or where in the hell it came from. They're puzzled."

"What about Gloria? Any news on her?"

"No ma'am, nothing, but we are doing are best to try and locate her."

"Okay, thanks for letting us know, sheriff."

"No problem," said Sheriff Wilson, hanging up the phone.

Tanya was nearly convinced that the Pavor Nocturnus was indeed real. She went back into her bedroom, and she continued to read.

With every chapter she read, she couldn't help but feel like this dark being was now a part of their lives, and it needed to be stopped. The book described how the creature would massacre someone and claim his or her soul. Sometimes it would take the person and their blood into its dark realm, making it look as if they vanished without a trace. Other times it would frame a person by killing its victims and leave a bloody mess behind. Mike stated in the book that his dad was framed for the murders of the three kids. He explained how it was a supernatural creature that covered its tracks so well that it was never caught.

Tanya was on chapter fifteen when the doorbell rang. She opened it, and Michael was at the door.

"Hi, sweetie, how was your day?"

"It was okay. Mom, it really smells gross in here still." Michael put his backpack down and headed into the kitchen to grab a snack from the pantry. Tanya followed behind him.

"I know. I'll light some more incense. Well, it is somebody's birthday tomorrow," she said with a smile.

"Phillip can still stay overnight, right Mom?"

Tanya remembered her promise to Michael, and after everything he had been through there was no way she could tell him no. "Yes, sweetie but I want you both in bed early, and promise me that you will keep your bedroom door locked. And please don't tell him about the monster."

"I promise I will keep the door locked. Can I go outside and play now?" asked Michael as he finished eating his Twinkie.

"I bet you can guess what I am going to ask you before I ask it," answered Tanya.

"Do I have homework, right?"

"Do you?"

"Yes, a little bit."

"Then you know what to do, right?"

"Can I do it later, Mom? Please?"

"Now mister."

"Okay, fine." Michael yanked his backpack from off the floor and threw one strap around his shoulder.

Michael ran upstairs with his backpack. He sat at his desk to do his homework and noticed it smelled like paint. When he turned toward the smell, he saw the repaired hole in his wall. It looked almost as if the hole never existed in the first place. Michael smiled as he looked at the patch job.

Tanya put a load of laundry into the washer and lit more incense. Afterward she smoked the entire house again with sage. Michael asked what she was doing when she entered his room with a bundle of burning sage in her hand. "I'm burning this to keep evil away," she told him.

"You mean the monster?"

"Yes."

"I hope it works."

"Me too," said Tanya under her breath. She left to go read more of her terrifying book.

# Chapter 17 The Ghost of Maya Collin's

After Michael finished his homework, he went outside to play by his favorite tree. He picked up a stick and started swinging it on an old black burnt tree stump he had found a few days ago. Every time he came outside to play, he would train for an hour and a half on the tree stump pretending it was The Pavor Nocturnus. Then he would visit Maya's grave, and afterward he would play in her favorite tree. Michael practiced doing a jump spinning slash with his stick. He gripped the stick firmly in his hand and spun into the air, coming down hard onto a thick, burnt branch coming out of the stump. The branch broke off and fell to the ground.

"Take that, you foul thing," he said, looking down at the broken branch he imagined was the monster's head. He skipped back to the gravestone and kneeled down on one knee in front of it. "Hi Maya," he said.

"Hi, Michael," said a lovely voice from behind him.

Startled, he grabbed his stick and quickly turned to face the voice. There before him stood Maya's ghost.

"It's okay, Michael. You don't have to be afraid. I won't hurt you." She opened up her arms, and the wind picked up as she took a deep breath in. Butterflies swarmed around them as the wind softly blew. "See? It is safe here."

"Yeah, I really like it here too," he said, feeling more at peace now.

"You know, you handle that thing pretty well."

"You mean this?" Michael held the stick high in the air.

"Yes, I have been watching you."

"How come I didn't see you?"

"The only time I am able to reveal myself to you is when you are in need of my aid."

"Are you a real ghost?"

"Yes, my physical body is no longer here, but my spiritual body will always be a part of this tree," she told him. "Now Michael I need you to listen to me carefully."

"Okay," said Michael, anxious to hear what she had to say.

"Did you know just how special you are?"

"No, why am I special?"

"You're special because you are able to wear that medallion without any problem. That medallion you wear around your neck is very old and very special, Michael. It is one of a kind, and it holds more power than any other object in the world. It holds so much good and so much love and peace. It can even grant miracles. However not just any person can wear it."

"What do you mean?" asked Michael.

"In other words, the person does not get to choose to wear it, but instead it gets to choose the person who wears it."

"Why?"

"Well, when I was a little girl, I had a friend named Martha Mayberry, and she loved the medallion so much that every day she begged and begged me to let her try it on, so I finally gave in one day and put it around her neck. She screamed and screamed for me to take it off. The medallion had burned a hole in her chest, so I took it off of her quickly."

"Oh no. Was she okay?" asked Michael.

"Yes, she was okay, but it did hurt her, and I felt absolutely terrible. After that day I was not allowed to play with Martha anymore."

"Why? It wasn't your fault."

"Well, it sort of was in a way, because the Archangel Michael told me never to take it off."

"So why did you give it to Mike?"

"I gave to Mike because he's my son, and my heart told me that he would soon need it."

"You didn't think it would burn him?"

"The thought didn't even cross my mind," said Maya's ghost. "The medallion chose him just as it chose you."

"I think I understand. I was able to use it to hurt the monster and so was Mike."

"Yes, that is right. That medallion you possess has the ability to call upon the Archangel Michael to aid you. Now I don't want you to be afraid Michael. What I am about to tell you is scary, but you must know this. Is that okay with you, Michael?"

"Yes, you can tell me."

"You and my Mike are two of the bravest boys in this world. The monster that you both have faced is not just a monster or night terror, Michael, but an ancient demon from a dark abyssal dimension completely void of light. My Mike hurt it with the medallion, and it has been hiding ever since. When you and your family moved in, it decided to target you." "But I hurt it with the medallion the other night," said Michael.

"True, you did hurt it, but now it is getting stronger, and it will come again soon."

"How is it getting stronger? What does it want from me?"

"I hate to be the bringer of such bad news, but you must know. When the Pavor Nocturnus kills a person, it takes their soul as well. An adult soul gives it power while a child's soul gives it much more because it is more pure. It has already killed three children and taken their souls. All it needs is the souls of six children, then it can come into this world day or night using any object no matter what color it is. There will be no way of stopping it after that."

"How do I stop it?"

"You are so very brave, young child. The only way to stop it for good is to call upon the aid of the Archangel Michael using that medallion. But once you do, you must fight it."

"How am I supposed to fight something like that? It is so scary, strong, and powerful. I am so scared, Maya." Michael started to cry.

"I can't imagine how hard this must be for you, Michael. But you are very strong and very brave and the Pavor Nocturnus knows it. You are the only one who can defeat this thing, as you now possess the medallion. I am afraid it is also targeting someone else in your family, not just you."

"Who else does it want?"

"In order to thrive in this world, it needs a soul so pure that it can survive."

"What does that mean? Who else does it want?"

"Your unborn sister," said Maya.

"No, it can't. I won't let it take her."

"My son gave you that medallion for a reason. Use it to stop the Pavor Nocturnus before it is too late."

"But how; what must I do to stop it from coming back?"

"You will know what to do when the time comes. Listen to your heart, Michael, and don't be afraid. You can defeat this thing. I have faith in you." Maya walked into her tree and vanished. Suddenly Tanya showed up at the tree.

"Hey mister, I thought I said two hours not three. Did you not look at your watch?" Tanya yelled.

"I'm sorry, Mom. I lost track of time."

"Well now you can do the dishes after dinner."

"Oh, come on, Mom," said Michael.

"Next time you will keep better track of time. It's getting dark. Let's go. Dinner is ready and Dad's home."

"What's for dinner?"

"Cheese cannelloni."

"Yum."

*****

After dinner, Michael did the dishes and sat down with Ron on the black leather couch to watch some television.

"You know, honey. Even with all of the windows open and the incense burning, it smells pretty bad," said Ron.

"Well, we will be out of here soon."

"Soon couldn't come soon enough," said Ron.

"Tell me about it," she said heading into the laundry room.

"Come on, little Tyson. Let's go beat on the bag a bit."

"Sure, Dad," said Michael, following him outside.

Tanya finished folding the laundry. She put the folded clothes into a basket and went upstairs to read more of her book. She left the basket of clean folded laundry next to her bed. The Dark Stalker was all about Mike Collins' encounters with the monster and the three boys it killed, however it also killed several other people at a dinner party. It also came after Mike Collins's son Tyler. Mike killed it in the end with the same medallion that her son had around his neck. Tanya realized it was nearly 10 p.m. and went downstairs and told Michael it was bedtime. Tanya tucked him into bed while Ron put in a new surveillance tape. Tanya came into the room and told Ron what Sheriff Wilson told her earlier.

"So it wasn't shit on our fridge or Michael's dresser or my sofa?"

"No, they said it was of unknown origin. For fuck sake, can't you see what's going on here?"

"Yeah, some kind of monster is after our son, right?"

"Yeah, Ron there is. And I would appreciate it if you didn't speak to me like I'm some fucking idiot."

"Well you believe in this damn thing as much as he does. You're afraid of the truth, aren't you? I told you once, and I will tell you again that until I see it on this screen, then the truth is that there are no monsters."

*****

Michael lay in his bed pondering everything Maya's ghost had told him, hoping to God that he wouldn't have to face this monster again. He held his medallion tightly in his hand and once again recited the Archangel Michael's prayer. He fell asleep with the light on and Tigger in bed next to him.

His medallion started to glow.

Tanya woke up at around midnight feeling a little restless so she walked into the computer room and turned it on to see if she could find any more useful information about her house. She typed in her address and found the same article she had read earlier. She clicked on the page with the pictures of the three boys, and when she did, it showed the three boys, however, Nathan was missing his eyes, Brandon was missing his head, and Andrew was missing both of his arms and his lower jaw. He had lacerations on his face and half of his neck had been eaten away. She screamed and turned off the monitor screen quickly. Frightened she slowly lifted her finger working up the courage to push the on button, and when she turned it back on, the kids were back to normal.

"Fuck this," she said. "I am going back to bed." She turned off the monitor and when she reached down to turn off the computer, she saw the Pavor Nocturnus hanging halfway out of it. It hissed at her and she awoke quickly, trying to catch her breath. She held onto Ron tightly and eventually fell back asleep.

# Chapter 18 Early Morning Surprises

The next day Tanya and Ron woke Michael up singing Happy Birthday. It was only 4 a.m. and it was still dark outside, but Ron insisted on giving Michael his present before he left for work.

"Wake up, sleepy head. I have a surprise for you downstairs," said Ron.

Michael put on his glasses and jumped out of bed. He ran downstairs, and there in the living room was a brand new Redline BMX bike.

"Wow. Thanks Mom. Thanks Dad. This is just what I wanted." He gave them both a big hug. "Can I ride it? Can I ride it, please?"

"Sure, go ahead," said Ron.

"Do you think that's a good idea, babe? It is still dark outside," said Tanya.

"He will be fine. Just stay close to the house."

"Okay, be careful though sweetie," said Tanya. "Go and put on some shoes and a jacket first." Michael ran off to get his shoes and jacket. "I'm going back to bed," she told Ron after she lit some incense and opened up all the windows. Whatever was rotting was creating the worst smell ever, and there were lots of flies in the house. Most of them were in the TV room where the smell seemed to be coming from.

Michael came racing down the stairs and wheeled his new chrome bike outside. It was still dark, so he ran back into the house and got a flashlight and some electric tape from the garage. He taped the flashlight to the handlebars on his bike and turned it on. He raced down the dirt path to Maya's tree. He was pedaling as fast as he could. He went up a dirt hill and down the other side then launched off a dirt jump at the bottom. Just as he did, Pavor Nocturnus rose from a dark puddle just below him, catching the frame of his bike in its hand, and lifting it high into the air with Michael still on it. He screamed as the monster flung him into the air while still holding onto his bike with its long black arm. Michael flew into the air and landed hard in the dirt. As he tried to catch his breath, he felt something cold trickling down his arm. He looked down at his elbow and noticed that it was bleeding. The hard dirt had taken his skin right off. He felt around for his glasses that fell off, and he grabbed them up and put them on quickly. He fixed his gaze on the demon who was staring right at him with blood red eyes. The monster threw Michael's bike aside, and it immediately went after him. Michael froze with fear for a second as Pavor Nocturnus started to walk toward him. Terrified he yelled, "Dad, help." His adrenaline took over, and he jumped to his feet and ran as fast as he could away from the hellish demon that was quickly advancing on him

Ron heard Michael's scream from inside the house. Tanya woke as he grabbed his bat from the bedroom.

"What happened?" she asked.

"Michael's in trouble." He ran down the stairs and out the door. Tanya grabbed the .38 Crystal had given her and slipped into some jeans and shoes. She ran as fast as she could to Maya's tree knowing in her heart that the tree was Michael's safe spot and the place he would most likely be.

Michael quickly climbed the tree and pointed his medallion at the monster that was now just a few feet from the tree. He started to recite the Archangel Michael's prayer but before he could finish, Pavor Nocturnus disappeared back into the shadows of the night and was gone. Michael cried as he held tightly onto Maya's tree. Ron found Michael's bike lying off the path in a bush, the flashlight still on.

"Oh no," said Ron as he continued to run along the path as fast as his two feet would take him. It was dark, and he tripped over a tree root. He fell to the dirt but quickly got back up. He yelled for Michael, and Michael yelled for his dad. Ron eventually found him hiding up in a big tree crying.

"What in the hell happened, slugger? Why are you up in that tree?"

"The monster picked me up while I was still on my bike, and he threw me off it. I scraped myself bad." Michael climbed down from the tree and showed his dad his ripped pajama bottoms and badly scraped knee.

"What did you do?"

"I ran up the tree, and the monster disappeared into the ground."

"Let's go home. I want you to take a shower and clean that wound with soap," Ron told him.

"You believe me though, right?"

"Show me where the monster grabbed you."

Michael started walking back to where the creature attacked him. Tanya was already there. She ripped the flashlight off the bike and used it to look at the bike. She noticed that smelly, slimy, dark residue on the frame of the bike and grabbed the .38 special from her back pocket as she headed for Maya's tree. She spotted something very tall and dark on the path, so she cocked the hammer back and pointed the gun at the figure in the distance. When it got closer, she could tell it was Ron carrying Michael on his shoulders. Tanya quickly but carefully un-cocked the hammer and put the gun back into the right back pocket of her jeans. "What the hell happened?" she asked.

Michael got down from his dad's shoulder and ran to Tanya. He laid his head on her shoulder and cried.

"It's okay now, honey. It's gone," she told him as she held him. "Oh no, Michael, your elbow is bleeding, sweetie." Tanya looked down at the wound.

Michael got back onto Ron's shoulders.

"Okay. Now show me where it attacked you."

Michael led his parents back to where the monster grabbed him. "He came out of this puddle here, lifting me up on my bike. And I landed over there." Ron glanced over at the puddle.

"You have got to stop lying to us, Michael."

"I'm not, Dad. I swear it."

Tanya pointed out the same smelly residue on the frame of the bike that Ron had found on the fridge.

"What in the hell is this nasty stuff?" asked Ron.

"It's some sort of secreted residue the monster leaves behind when it comes into this world. But it can only come through something black or dark," said Tanya.

"Oh yeah?" said Ron.

"Uh huh," said Michael.

"So what makes you the expert, Tanya?" asked Ron.

"'The Dark Stalker,' by Mike Collins."

"Can we go back home now? It's not safe here," said Michael.

"Okay, but first let me take a closer look at the puddle where you claim this thing attacked you," said Ron. Michael pointed down at the puddle of black stagnant water that was just below a dirt jump. Tanya grabbed a stick and stirred it then pulled the stick out of the water and put it up to Ron's nose.

"Ugh. Gross. Knock it off, Tanya. That shit is foul," said Ron.

"It's monster slime. Can we go home now, Dad?" asked Michael.

"Okay." Ron grabbed Michael's bike. He wheeled it back to the house while Tanya held Michael's hand and walked him back to the house using the flashlight as a guide.

Once they arrived back at the house, Tanya took a closer look at Michael's cuts. Ron sent him upstairs to take a shower and clean up his elbow and knee with soap then said to Tanya, "Since you seem to know so much about this monster, can you tell me where in the hell it came from?"

"Well, that is one guess," she said.

"What is?"

"Hell," replied Tanya, "but in Mike Collins' book he said it came from an extremely dark abyssal realm completely absent of any good or light."

"That is pretty disturbing. But why in God's name is it after our son?"

"I have no idea. Maybe because his name is Michael too or maybe there is a link between our Michael, Mike Collins, and The Archangel Michael."

"That sounds ridiculous, but those kids I saw the other night scared the hell out of me."

"They scared me half to death too," said Tanya.

"When he said it was real I completely lost it. I want to believe Michael about it, and hell maybe I am starting to now. But this whole situation everything that's happened, I mean what could it possibly want from us or from Michael?"

"I don't know, babe, and I don't want to know. I just want to stop the fucking thing before it hurts or kills us."

"Okay, so tell me, how would you stop something like this, Tanya?"

Before she could answer him, Michael came downstairs wearing nothing but a towel wrapped around his lower half and the Archangel's medallion around his neck. "Mom, I don't have any clean underwear," he said.

"Okay, I will be right back." Tanya walked upstairs. Ron noticed the medallion around Michael's neck.

"That's neat, slugger." Ron reached out and grabbed for the medallion with his fingers.

"Dad, don't," said Michael, but it was too late. The medallion burned Ron's fingers. "Ouch, fuck," Ron yelled, pulling his hand away.

Tanya came back downstairs, and as she handed Michael his underwear, he grabbed them and quickly ran upstairs.

"What happened?" she asked.

"I went to grab the medallion on his neck, and it burned the holy fuck out of my hand like it had been sitting in a lit fire all night."

"Well, there is your answer," said Tanya, walking to the freezer. She handed Ron an ice pack for his hand.

"What the fuck is that supposed to mean?"

"That medallion is the answer to stopping that evil thing once and for all."

"Michael, come down here," yelled Ron.

Michael ran downstairs. Ron asked him where he got the medallion and how it worked. Michael told him everything. However, he did not mention to him that the monster was after his soul as well as that of his unborn sister.

"So let me get this right. You were chosen to stop this monster using that medallion that was given to you by Mike Collins, and angels in Heaven made it. It was given to his mom Maya by not just an angel but also the Archangel Michael himself. You know, slugger, that story is about as hard to swallow as a jar of nails," said Ron.

"I swear it is true, Dad," said Michael.

"I believe you, sweetie," said Tanya.

"Of course you do," said Ron. "We'll see soon enough if this thing is real, but I doubt it."

Tanya lit some more incense, and Ron gave Michael a kiss on the head. "Well happy birthday, slugger. I'm sorry you had a rough morning, but you do know that I love you more than anything, right slugger?"

"Yeah, I know. I love you too, Dad." Ron rubbed the top of his head. Michael got ready for school and gave Tanya a hug.

"Happy birthday sweetie, have a good day in school," she told him.

"I will," he said as he rushed out the door to catch the bus. He was still a bit shook up from his encounter with the monster. But he was also excited about his new bike and also that it was his birthday and Phillip was staying the night tonight.

Later that morning, Tanya walked back to where Michael had been attacked by the Pavor Nocturnus. When she came to the puddle, she noticed some strange large footprints with claws on the end of them. They led all the way to Maya's tree. Tanya knew what they belonged to. It started to rain hard, and she rushed back to the house.

# Chapter 19 Michael's Birthday Party

At lunchtime, Phillip told Michael that he would be at his house at around 4 p.m. with the wooden swords and shields and that if he were lying about the monster, he would beat him with the wooden sword.

"Okay, but if you see it, then the sword and shield are mine," said Michael.

"You got yourself a deal, liar," said Phillip.

"Okay, you'll see."

"Yeah, I'll see you lose this bet."

"Keep telling yourself that."

"I sure will, and you will be the sore loser after I get done beating you with my sword."

Michael ignored Phillip's comments, knowing he would soon see the truth for himself. After Michael got home from school, he went up to the computer room to play with his toys. Every couple of minutes he would gaze out the window to see if Phillip had arrived. Tanya kept thinking about the possible dangers that could arise during the night. However, she kept good on her promise not to upset Michael on his birthday by telling him that Phillip could not stay the night.

When Phillip arrived, Michael ran outside to greet him. Phillip had a big duffle bag in his arms.

"Happy birthday, Michael," Sandra said as she handed him a card.

"Thank you, Sandra," said Michael with a big smile.

"You two have fun. Phillip, you be good for Mrs. Walker," said Sandra.

"Yeah, sure, whatever," said Phillip as Sandra waved goodbye to them.

Tanya introduced herself. "Hi, Phillip. I'm Tanya, Michael's mom."

"Hi," said Phillip to Tanya, in a rather dull voice. Tanya walked up to Sandra's car. Sandra rolled down her window.

"Hi, Sandra, it's good to see you again."

"Likewise, and thank you so much for watching him. He can be a bit overwhelming for me."

"Don't worry. It's my pleasure. He is all Michael could talk about this week, so I am happy to have him."

"Well, I am certainly glad he has made a new friend. Michael is such a wonderful boy, Tanya."

"Thank you. That sure warms my heart to hear."

"I should be by to pick him up around three tomorrow, unless Michael wants him to stay another night, and that would be fine with me too."

"Okay. We will see how it goes, and I will call you to let you know unless you call me first," said Tanya.

"Will do. Thanks again. See you later." Sandra as she drove off.

"Did you fart, Michael?" asked Phillip as he entered the house. "No, Tigger killed something and hid it in the TV room somewhere, and now we can't find it," said Michael.

"Eww, gross," said Phillip, holding his nose.

Tanya lit some incense and candles.

"Come on. I'll show you my room," said Michael, walking up the stairs. Once they got into Michael's room, Phillip told Michael to open his card, and he did. The card said "Happy Birthday" on the front, and when Michael opened the card, a twenty-dollar bill fell to the floor. Phillip picked it up and put it in his pocket. Before Michael could finish reading his card, Phillip ripped it from out his hand and tore it to pieces.

"Why the hell did you do that?" Michael asked.

"You don't want that. You want this," said Phillip, waving the twenty-dollar bill in the air.

Michael snatched it out of Phillip's hand.

"Show me where this monster came from?" asked Phillip.

Michael pointed at his dresser and told him, "It came out of the top of that dresser before I painted it white."

"What color was it before?"

"Black. That's the color the monster uses to come into our world."

"Well you did a lousy fucking job painting it."

"Yeah, well at least it can't get me from there anymore."

"You're so full of shit your eyes are brown."

"No they're not. They're blue, dumb ass."

"Whatever. There is no stupid monster though."

"Just wait. You'll see for yourself soon enough, but we have to wait for my parents to go to sleep first. They'll be watching us on the security cameras too."

"Cool. Do you have a security camera in your room? Where is it?"

"There is one in the hallway and two downstairs, but I don't have one in my room."

"What do you have security cameras for?"

"I did it so that my parents could see the monster for themselves."

"What? They think you are a liar too?"

"Well my mom believes me, but my dad doesn't."

"Did she see it or something?"

"She has seen the ghosts of the children that were murdered here. And the slime the monster leaves behind."

"And what about your dad?" asked Phillip.

"He has seen them too. And the slime. But he still doesn't believe it's real."

"That's because it isn't real. You probably used some of that black slime you can get at Kay Bee Toys."

"It attacked me on my bike this morning, and I messed up my knee bad."

"You probably crashed your bike because you can't ride it."

"You'll believe me soon enough," said Michael.

A sound like a hundred faucets all turned on at once came from outside, and as Michael gazed out the window, he saw that it was pouring rain. Phillip and Michael stayed inside and watched TV.

"Hey, Birthday Boy," Ron exclaimed when he got home. "How was your day?"

"It was okay I guess."

"Okay? Only okay? Well that just won't do," said Ron. "I got something that might cheer you up." He walked upstairs to his bedroom, and when he came back downstairs with Tanya, he was holding a box in blue wrapping paper with a blue bow on top. Tanya was holding a smaller present wrapped in the same blue wrapping paper and a card.

Tanya handed him the card. "Happy birthday, sweetie."

Michael opened it and read it. "Thanks Mom. Thanks Dad," said Michael giving them both a big hug. He opened the large present first. It was a brand new PlayStation. "Wow, this is awesome. Thank you so much."

"You're a spoiled brat," said Phillip.

"Shut up, Phillip," said Michael. He opened the other gift, and it was Tekken 2. "Awesome," said Phillip. "Let's play it."

"Thanks a million. You guys are the best," said Michael, giving them both another big hug.

"You're welcome. We both thought you earned it," said Ron.

"I hope you enjoy it, sweetie," said Tanya.

Ron set it up for the boys to play in the TV room. "Honey, can you light some more incense? I'm going out to get pizza."

"Sure, babe." Tanya lit two sticks. She placed one on the television and the other on the table then sprayed Lysol throughout the room and killed some more flies that were lingering around the television.

"Quit farting, Michael. You stink," said Phillip.

"Whatever," said Michael, knocking Phillip's jaguar character out with a powerful punch. "Take that, you stupid animal," said Michael.

"Fuck you, cheater," said Phillip.

"Hey, watch your language in there," said Tanya.

After Michael beat Phillip nearly a dozen times, Ron returned with the pizza.

"Cool, let's eat," said Michael.

"Whatever, you suck," said Phillip, throwing down the PlayStation controller.

After dinner Ron, Tanya, and Phillip sang "Happy Birthday" to Michael. Phillip's version ended with "Happy birthday to you, you eat lots of poo, you are a dumb fart face, and you smell like shit too."

"Don't talk to my son like that in my house," said Ron, "unless you want a fresh one." He showed Phillip the back of his hand.

"Didn't your mom teach you any manners?" said Tanya.

"Okay. I'm sorry, Mr. and Mrs. Walker. It won't happen again."

"Good," said Ron. "Now let's have some cake."

After they finished eating, Ron and Tanya cleaned up and did the dishes.

Phillip told Michael, "Your parents are assholes." Michael punched him in the stomach, knocking him to the ground. "Hey, I was just joking, Hercules." Phillip tried to catch his breath.

"If you say one more bad thing about my parents, I swear I will never speak to you again," said Michael.

"All right, I won't. I promise."

They returned to playing Tekken 2.

"I play the winner," said Ron as he watched Michael beat the living shit out of Phillip. He grabbed the controller from Phillip's hand. "All right, Phillip. This is how it's done." Ron picked Jack, and Michael picked Paul. Michael went to do his special power punch move, but Ron jumped over it, and they exchanged punches. Ron won the first round, and Michael won the second round, then Ron won the fight.

"My turn now," said Phillip, picking King.

Ron got a flawless victory for the first round, and in the second round, he beat Phillip. They played back and forth for hours until Tanya said, "its bedtime, boys."

"Just one more fight," said Michael. "Please Mom."

"It's 11:00. Bedtime. Now," said Tanya loudly.

"Okay, Mom," said Michael. The boys put on their pajamas and went into Michael's room.

Ron put in another tape and hit Record. Ron and Tanya watched to see if the boys would stay in their room. "You know, now I know why Mike punched that kid," said Ron to Tanya.

"He was rude, wasn't he?" said Tanya.

"Yeah, if I said something like that as a kid my dad would have knocked my block off," said Ron.

"He also called Michael a fucking cheater in the living room because he was kicking his ass at the game," said Tanya.

"Hell, he was kicking my ass at the game too," said Ron. He grabbed Tanya and kissed her goodnight. He fell asleep shortly after while Tanya watched the monitor for a little bit. The boys remained in the room, so she lay down in her bed while staring at the clear, sparkling, beautiful, crystal on her bed stand wondering how Crystal's date with Sean was going.

# Chapter 20 No Such Thing as Monsters

"Michael, do you think your parents are asleep yet?" asked Phillip.

"I'm not sure. Maybe we should wait a little bit longer," said Michael.

"Okay but in five minutes I'm leaving this room and you're going to show me this so called monster, right?"

"I don't think this is such a good idea."

"I knew you were fucking lying to me. There is no stupid monster, is there?"

"No, there really is a monster, Phillip, but it's very dangerous and scary. It kills and eats kids."

"Well, then you take this." Phillip handed Michael a wooden sword and shield. "I'll grab mine. You lead the way."

Michael carefully opened the bedroom door, and very quietly, they walked downstairs. "The cameras can see us." Michael pointed to the low-hanging camera facing the kitchen. Phillip walked up to the camera, picked his nose, and rubbed a big booger on the cameras lens. "You're such an asshole."

"And you're a fucking liar. Where is this fake monster at?"

"Shh.. be quiet. You'll wake up my parents."

Michael and Phillip crept into the kitchen.

"All right. Where is it?" Michael pointed to the fridge. "Oh give me a break." Phillip opened the refrigerator door. "You expect me to believe there's a real monster living inside your fridge? What a joke. You know? You are the sorriest fucking liar on earth." He closed the refrigerator door. "I never believed you anyway, because there's no such thing as monsters." A large black hand with pointy sharp fingers reached out of the black fridge and gripped Phillip's neck. Phillip dropped his sword and shield and tried to pry apart the monster's fingers. The Pavor Nocturnus stuck its evil head out of the fridge and bared its teeth to him as it hissed and growled. Phillip peed himself as the monster stared at him with its devil red eyes and its evil grin. It pulled Phillip into the fridge. He disappeared.

Michael stood frozen in shock until Phillip's head and face came halfway out of the fridge. His mouth was open. He was screaming, his head covered in the smelly black residue and his eyes bloodshot. Suddenly the screams stopped, and the rest of Phillip's severed head came out of the center of the fridge door and fell onto the floor. Michael dropped his sword and shield onto the floor and screamed.

*****

Tanya heard Michael's scream and turned on her light. Her beautiful clear crystal was now completely gloss black. She grabbed the .38 from her dresser drawer and put it into the pocket of her nightgown then dashed down the stairs. Ron was still in a deep sleep snoring loudly.

*****

The Pavor Nocturnus reached its hand out from the bottom half of the black fridge and grabbed Phillip's severed head before pulling it back into the fridge. Tanya came running into the kitchen. She pulled out the gun and turned on the light. Michael grabbed onto her crying.

"The monster killed Phillip," he said.

"What do you mean, the monster killed Phillip?"

"It ripped off his head and pushed it through the fridge." Michael cried.

"Where is his head?" Tanya was freaked out.

"He took it." Michael sobbed.

"What do you mean? Took it where?"

"He grabbed Phillip by his neck and pulled him into the fridge. His head fell out of the fridge, and the monster pulled it back in."

Tanya opened the fridge. Nothing was inside it but food and drinks. Stinky slime covered the center and lower half of the fridge as well as the floor where Michael said Phillip's head had fallen. But there was no blood. Michael trembled.

*****

Tanya went upstairs and woke up Ron. She explained to him what Michael had just seen.

"You're fucking kidding me," said Ron. "Please tell me you are fucking joking."

"Look at my crystal, Ron. Does it look like I am fucking joking?"

"Holy shit. What the fuck is that?"

He took his pocketknife and tried to scrape at the crystal.

"The fucking monster killed Phillip in our kitchen, Ron, and our son saw it happen. Look at him. He's scared to death."

"What exactly happened, Michael?" Ron asked. Michael couldn't talk.

Tanya showed Ron the slime and explained to him word for word what Michael had told her.

"Okay, I have to check the tape right now." Ron ran upstairs and rewound the tape.

"I can't live here anymore," Tanya said as she picked up the phone. "I'm calling Crystal." She answered right away. She was giggling. "Hi, Crystal, It's Tanya. Am I interrupting anything?"

"We're caught. Say 'hi,' Sean. It's Tanya."

"Hi, Tanya," said Sean in the background.

"Hi, Sean."

"Is everything alright, sweetie?" Crystal asked. "Did you want to come over with Michael and stay the night?"

"I don't mind," said Sean.

"See. Sean doesn't mind either. Come on over."

"No. It's okay. I was just calling to see how your date went," said Tanya.

"It went better than I expected," said Crystal.

"I can see that. I'm sorry for disturbing you two."

"Are you sure everything is okay, hun?"

"Yeah, everything is fine. I'll see you tomorrow."

"Okay. I can't wait. I love you."

"I love you too," said Tanya and hung up. "I can't take this anymore," she said crying and hugging Michael.

"It's okay, Mom. I'll protect you." Michael picked up his sword and shield.

"I know you will, sweetie," said Tanya giving him a hug. The baby kicked. "Did you feel that?" she asked Michael with a smile.

"I sure did," said Michael with a big smile. "I won't let anything happen to you two."

"That little bastard," yelled Ron from the living room.

"What is it, babe?" asked Tanya.

"Come here. I'll show you."

Ron was rewinding the tape when Michael and Tanya entered the living room. The tape showed Phillip walk up to the camera, pick a big booger from his nose, and wipe it on the camera lens. Michael called him an asshole. Michael laughed and so did Tanya.

"Well, I'm glad you two think this is so damn funny," Ron said.

When he saw Michael and Tanya head into the kitchen, he heard Phillip say, "You know? You are the sorriest fucking liar on earth."

"Can you believe the mouth on this kid?" said Ron. The sound faded, so he turned up the volume on the TV. He heard Phillip's wooden sword and shield hit the floor and turned the volume up even more. After a few seconds, Ron and Tanya both heard the monster for the first time, and Ron paused the tape. "Michael, was that what I think it was?" asked Ron.

"Yes, Dad, it was the monster. Now do you believe me?"

Ron pushed Play on the VCR again and seconds later, he heard Phillip screaming.

"I can't listen to this anymore," said Tanya. She and Michael went upstairs. Ron continued to listen, and after Phillip's screams ceased, he heard what he could only assume was Phillip's severed head hitting the floor. He heard Michael's sword and shield hit the floor and Michael scream. Shortly after, he saw Tanya run downstairs and into the kitchen. He could also hear Michael tell her everything that had just happened. Based on the sounds and noises Ron had just heard, he knew Michael was telling the truth.

Ron opened the fridge, pulled everything out, and set it all on the kitchen counter and table. He grabbed his white king-size bed sheet from the cupboard and went back into the kitchen. He turned the light on and looked at the fridge as if the monster were coming out of it, and quickly threw the white bed sheet over it. He went into the garage, grabbed a large dolly with straps, and brought it inside. He moved the fridge out of its corner, unplugged it, and loaded it onto the dolly. He opened the sliding glass door and wheeled it into the back yard and around the side by the gate. He went back inside and put the rest of the food into the white fridge in the garage then went upstairs to bed. Tanya and Michael were holding onto each other fast asleep.

"I believe you now, son." He rubbed Michael's head and lay down with his baseball bat next to him, staring at the monitor until he could no longer keep his eyes open.

The next morning Ron woke at 7:00, called his boss, and told him he had a family emergency and would be in at noon. He let Tanya and Michael rest as he grabbed Sheriff Wilson's card from his wallet and called him.

"Hi, this is Sheriff Wilson. How can I help you?"

"Yeah, this is Ron Walker from the old Collins residence."

"Oh yeah, I remember you. What can I do you for?"

"I need to speak with you now, at my house, in person."

"Okay. What's the emergency?"

"I have to show you something important."

"What is this all about?"

"I think a boy was murdered here last night by the same thing that left that slime on my fridge."

"You stay put. I'll be there in ten minutes."

Ron opened up all the windows in the house and lit five sticks of incense then sprayed Lysol throughout the house. He rewound the videotape to where the boys came downstairs. Sheriff Wilson arrived quickly and told Ron to take a seat.

"You're not going to try any weird voodoo on me with all that incense burning are you?" asked Sheriff Wilson.

"No. I'm sorry my cat Tigger killed something outside and decided he would hide it somewhere in the house."

"So you said a boy was murdered here last night?"

"Yes, I think so."

"Why in the hell wouldn't you call me when it happened?"

"Because I was looking over the security tape to see exactly what happened."

"Okay. What was this boy's name?"

"His name was Phillip Gibbons."

"Oh, I'm familiar with that one," said Sheriff Wilson.

"How do you know him?"

"He set fire to his teacher's house a few years back, and he likes to set cats on fire and shove firecrackers up their assholes and light them."

"I'm glad Tigger slept outside last night."

"Yeah, he is a bad seed and his dad was even worse."

"How so?"

"Well I hauled his ass in last year for a murder charge and he had prior's like battery, robbery, arson and the rape of an underage girl."

"Holy shit. I had his kid stay at my house last night."

"Apparently. Can you show me exactly what happened?"

"Yeah, sure." Ron pushed Play on the VCR, and Sheriff Wilson watched the entire tape. Ron explained to him that Michael saw a monster kill Phillip. "So what do you think?"

"I think you are up to something. Does Mrs. Gibbons know about her son?"

"No sir, I called you first thing when I woke up. But come on, let's be real. You heard that growl and those screams, and you should know by watching the video that none of us could have killed him."

"No, I don't know that you couldn't have poisoned him, or set some kind of sick trap to make it look like an accident. Or hell, your son could have done it. Where is he by the way?"

"He's upstairs in our room asleep with his mom."

"I would like to go up and have a word with both of them if you don't mind."

"Sure. I'll come with you."

"No, you will stay right there on that couch until I get back."

"Okay, fine."

Sheriff Wilson woke them.

"What in the hell . . . Where is my husband?" said Tanya.

"He's downstairs on the couch. Now what can you tell me about Phillip Gibbons, Michael. And don't you lie to me, boy."

"The Pavor Nocturnus killed him last night in the kitchen."

"What killed him?"

"The Night Terror," said Tanya. "It's a monster that lives in this house, and it killed the three children Nathan, Andrew, and Brandon back in 1976. It killed Phillip and probably Gloria too. And now it's after my son."

"Robert Collins was the monster that killed those kids back in 1976," said Sheriff Wilson.

"How would you know? You weren't there," said Tanya.

"No. But my daddy was here and that crazy son of a bitch hacked them to bits with an axe."

"Well there wasn't any blood on that axe, was there sheriff?" she asked. "And how could he rip somebody's jaw off with just his bare hands?"

"You would be surprised at what a psychopath is capable of," said Sheriff Wilson. "Not to mention that there are no such things as monsters. Robert was the real monster, and maybe your husband is too."

"Don't you dare call him a monster," Tanya cried. "You don't know the hell we have been put through by this thing."

"Babe, are you okay?" asked Ron walking into the room.

"I'm okay."

"I thought I told you to wait for me downstairs on the couch," said Sheriff Wilson. "Look if you are going to arrest me, do it already, but stop upsetting my wife and kid."

"All right, I will give you until tonight to show me some hard evidence on tape of this thing you say killed Phillip and Gloria. If you can't give me proof, I am hauling all three of you in. Got it?"

"Understood," said Ron.

"I'm also going to take this tape with me and review it some more."

"Fine, take it," said Ron.

"You folks have yourselves a nice day, and don't go anywhere." He tipped his hat down with his finger.

Ron saw him to the door, and Tanya watched him pull out of the driveway, flipping him the bird through the upstairs window.

"I swear if he didn't have that badge, I would have one two'd his ass right out of our house," said Ron. "I believe you now, Michael."

"You do really?"

"Yeah, I'm so sorry for doubting you." He gave him a big hug.

"Don't worry. We will stop it together. Right?" Michael asked.

"Do you know you are even braver than I am?" said Ron.

"Thanks, Dad. I love you."

"You're welcome, my little Mike Tyson. I love you too." Ron kissed his head. "Alright, babe. I have got to go to work now. And I promised Victor, Eddie, and Ralph that they could come over tonight, and we could drink some beers."

"Alright babe you deserve that, plus I promised Crystal that we would have a girl's night out anyway. But what about Sheriff Wilson?"

"Don't worry. I will handle him when he comes over. He doesn't have nothing on us anyway."

"Okay honey. Promise me you'll watch out for Michael and protect him if anything happens."

"Of course I will."

"Promise me you will, Ron."

"I promise you I won't let anything happen to our son," he said.

"Okay. Be careful sweetie." She gave him a kiss and hug. "I love you, Ronnie Walker."

"I love you too, babe. And don't worry, we'll be fine." He headed out the front door, and Tanya blew him a kiss from the upstairs window. He caught it in his right hand and put it over his heart and waved goodbye to her from his truck. Tanya lay back down in bed with Michael. Tanya looked at her onyx black crystal knowing it was the monster's doing.

Tanya woke from a long nap and woke Michael. By the time they both showered, it was almost 2 p.m. Once Ron got home at 5 p.m., she would leave to go to Crystal's house. Michael asked Tanya if he could go outside and play.

"Sure, honey, but I want you back here at 4:30 sharp."

 "Okay Mom."

"Honey, I want you to know that I am really sorry about your friend," said Tanya.

"It's okay. It's not your fault. He wouldn't believe me about the monster anyway."

"What do you mean? I thought I told you not to tell him about the monster."

"I told him about it when I went over to his house to play, but he just said there was no such thing as monsters."

The phone rang, and Michael went outside to play just as Tanya answered it. "Hi, Tanya," said the voice of an older woman on the phone,

"Hi. Uh, who is this?"

"It's Sandra, Phillip's mom."

Tanya's heart jumped into her chest. She was at a complete loss for words. She said the only thing that came to her." Hi, Sandra. How are you?"

"I'm good. Is Phillip there?"

"Yeah, but he is playing outside with Michael right now."

"Oh, okay. I have a quick question for you."

"Sure, what is it?" said Tanya horrified at what she might say next.

"I was wondering if it would be all right with you if Phillip stayed another night there with you guys."

"Sure," said Tanya. "We would love to have him."

"Great, you don't know how much I appreciate this. He can be a bit much for me to handle sometimes.

"Well, he has been great for us. It has been a pleasure having him, Sandra."

"That is sure nice to hear. It is rare that he is good to anyone. That's why I didn't mind that Michael gave him a good punch in the nose."

"Oh, I am so sorry about that," said Tanya.

"I am totally sure he deserved it, and if it was up to me, I would let you keep him forever."

"Well we just might," said Tanya shocked and surprised at what she just heard.

"Okay, tell him to be good, and I will get him sometime tomorrow afternoon. Will that be all right with you?"

"Yes that will be fine. You have a wonderful evening, Sandra."

"You do the same. Bye for now." Sandra hung up the phone.

"Holy shit," Tanya said. "What in the hell am I going to tell her tomorrow when she comes over? That her son was decapitated by a monster that came out of our fridge and then snatched him away into the abyss? I would be locked up for sure. Or maybe she would thank me. Who knows? Sheriff Wilson is right. We need some evidence of this monster or we are fucked."

# Chapter 21 Training Hard

Meanwhile, Michael rode his bike to Maya's tree. He brought a shovel and dug a hole in front of the tree to the left of Maya's tree. He rode his bike back home and grabbed Phillip's wooden sword and shield as well has his own. He put them all into Phillip's bag and rode back to the tree where he had dug the hole. He put Phillip's sword and shield in the hole and used the shovel to fill the hole. Then, he said a prayer for Phillip.

"Dear, God. I know that Phillip could be mean sometimes, but if you could please forgive him and let him into Heaven, I would be ever so grateful. And please, God, give me the strength and courage to defeat this monster so it can never ever try to hurt me or my family or friends again. I love you, Lord, and thank you for hearing and answering my prayers. In Jesus' name. Amen."

He made a cross using some electric tape and two sticks he had found. He stuck it in the ground and paid his respects to Maya as well. He slashed at the burnt tree hard and fast with his wooden sword and spun around, hitting the stump with his shield. The stump cracked halfway through and Michael kicked it hard enough to crack it in half. He stood over the burnt stump and thrust the tip of his wooden broadsword into it. He pulled it from the stump and said, "Now I'm ready."

*****

Ron brought home a few cases of beer around quarter past five. Tanya kissed him goodbye and told him to watch Michael. "I'll be home no later than 11," she said and gave Michael a kiss. "Be careful," she told him. She gave him her pager number. "If this thing comes back, I want you to page me. Put 911 after you put in our number so I know to come home quickly. OK?"

"Okay Mom. I will."

"You are so brave and strong, and growing up fast. I'm proud of you."

"Thanks Mom. I love you."

"I love you too, sweetie," she said and left for Crystal's house.

Ron put in a new tape and hit Record on his monitor. He also cleaned off the big booger that Phillip had smeared onto the cameras lens. "Thanks for that, Phillip," he said to himself. He killed a bunch of flies in the TV room and sprayed the rest of the Lysol can in the room to get rid of the terrible smell.

About an hour later Victor, Eddie, and Ralph showed up with two more cases of cold beer. The four of them went into the garage while Michael played Tekken 2 on the black leather sofa, his wooden shield and sword next to him. They all were listening to the radio and drinking beer and having a good old time playing poker. Ron tried as hard as he could to forget about the monster and Sheriff Wilson, but he knew that he needed evidence of this thing or else he might be charged for double murder.

"Is everything okay, Ron?" asked Ralph.

"Yeah. Everything is good. No worries."

"What's the matter, Ronnie boy? The wife not giving you any pussy?" said Victor laughing.

Ron shot up from his chair and knocked Victor out with one punch.

"Fuck you, Victor. You punk motherfucker. Get your bitch ass up. Who the fuck do you think you are disrespecting my wife like that in front of me? Get up."

"Relax Ron," said Ralph, holding him back.

"What the hell is the matter with you, Ron?" asked Eddie.

"What the hell is the matter with me? This prick says my wife isn't giving me any pussy, and you want to know what's wrong with me?"

Eddie woke Victor. Ron looked at him and said, "Don't you ever disrespect my wife in front of me again."

Eddie grabbed two beers from the fridge and they both walked inside the house. "Man, fuck Ron. I should go back out there and kick his ass," said Victor.

"Come on let's get out of here," said Eddie opening the sliding door. He and Victor walked out to the patio. "Are you okay, man? He hit you pretty fucking hard."

"I'm fine, and once I am done with this beer, I'm going back into the garage and knocking his fucking teeth in," said Victor.

"Shut up, Vic. You're drunk. Plus, he will kick your ass, and you know it."

"Man, fuck you, Eddie. Just watch. You'll see."

"Whatever, man. I've got to take a shit and have a piss," said Eddie and walked back inside the house.

"Well, fuck you then," said Victor. He turned his attention to Ron's punching bag. It was raining pretty hard outside and thundering. "All right, Ron. Let's do this," said Victor and dropped his half-empty beer bottle. He punched the bag with a left hook followed by a right hook and then swung a straight left as hard as he could. But before his punch connected with the bag, the Pavor Nocturnus grabbed hold of his hand from out of the black punching bag and tore it clean off. Victor screamed as blood poured from his wrist where his hand used to be. Neither Ron nor Michael heard his screams over the rain, thunder, radio, and television.

The outside light burst into shards of glass, and the monster's clawed hand rose from the top of the punching bag and used its razor sharp claws to cut the straps on top of it. The bag fell to the floor. Victor stepped back a few feet and the light came on again.

The Pavor Nocturnus crawled slowly out of the black bag. Victor couldn't believe what he was seeing. The terrifying creature stood up, and Victor ran for the fence. He tried to hop over it, but the monster pulled him off then picked him up by his head with both hands and lifted him high into the air. Victor screamed at the top of his lungs, but it was no use. The monster crushed his head like a watermelon. Blood, skull fragments, and brain matter went everywhere as Victor's lifeless corpse fell to the floor convulsing. The monster let out a loud roar and quickly crawled on all fours back into Ron's black bag. The light bulb went dead.

*****

Ron went inside to put Michael to bed. "Come on, slugger. It's bedtime."

Michael put down the controller, grabbed his sword and shield, and followed Ron upstairs.

"Listen, slugger. I want you to keep this door shut and locked. If you see any sign of this monster, I want you to come and get me right away. Do you hear me?"

"Yes, Dad."

Ron headed back to the garage.

# Chapter 22 "Monsters Do Exist"

When Eddie finished using the bathroom, he glanced outside and saw that the light was turned off, and Victor was gone. He heard a game playing in the TV room and sat down on the leather couch.

"Man, it fucking stinks in here," he said as he picked up the controller and started to play Tekken 2. He chose Yoshimitsu as a character, and was facing Martial Law. He lost both rounds and quickly grew bored with it, so he set the controller down. Ron's double bass caught his attention.

"What in the hell is this thing?" he said to himself as he opened the case. He pulled out the double bass.

"No fucking way," he said and stood it up while trying to play it. The light went out, and he heard loud static coming from the TV. When he looked at it, he could have sworn he saw the severed rotting head of an older woman inside it.

"What the fuck is that?" The static stopped, and Tekken 2 came back on. Eddie set the bass on the black leather couch. He took a close look at the screen, but it was just the game playing. A long black clawed arm came from out of the sofa, pulled out the largest steel string from the double bass, and yanked it into the couch.

"What the fuck was that?" said Eddie turning to see what just happened. The static noise came back, and when he looked at the TV, he briefly saw the severed head again, this time covered in maggots. Then Tekken 2 came back on.

"Man, I must be having acid flashbacks again," he said staring at the screen. A black arm reached up through the case of the double bass and pulled it shut. Eddie jumped to the side and stared at the closed case. He crept toward the large bass case and slowly opened it. There was nothing there.

"What o- ?" before he could finish the word, Pavor Nocturnus had come halfway out of the case and wrapped the bass string around Eddie's head and open mouth. The demon pulled the string as hard as it could, completely severing the top half of Eddie's head clean from his body. He bled profusely. His tongue moved inside of what was left of his head. The monster pulled the rest of his body into the bass case, and the lid slammed shut.

*****

Ron and Ralph were still in the garage playing cards when Ron heard a loud bang on his garage door. He opened it up and standing there in the pouring rain was Sheriff Wilson in a black raincoat. "I'm back. You got something for me?" he asked.

"Would you like a beer first?" asked Ron.

"Get inside, and show me the tape, and I swear if you don't have something for me, I'm going to take your ass in right now. You hear me, boy?"

Ron took a deep breath, trying hard not to lose it on Sheriff Wilson. "Yes, I hear you. Come inside, and I will show you."

Sheriff Wilson and Ralph followed Ron into the house. "Damn boy it smells like a dead whore's crotch in here," said Sheriff Wilson. "Where in the hell is that awful smell coming from?" He walked into the TV room and saw Tekken 2 playing on the screen. He noticed Ron's double bass lying on the couch and missing a string. Blood was all over the place, most of it on and around Ron's double bass case. Officer Wilson drew his gun and told Ron and Ralph to put their hands in the air. As soon as they did, the lid on Ron's bass case opened a few inches then closed quickly.

"What the fuck was that?" Sheriff Wilson turned and pointed his gun at the case. He slowly reached down and quickly opened the lid of the case. Inside of it was Eddie, hacked to bits, and covered in a smelly black slime like residue. His torso was completely severed in half, and his arms and legs had been cut clean off. His severed arm's hand was holding his penis, which had also been ripped off. The top half of his head was staring right up at Sheriff Wilson with dead bloodshot eyes and a bloody bass string lying next to it.

Sheriff Wilson pointed the gun back at Ron and told him to turn around. "I knew you were a sick fuck, but you are going to fucking fry for this, you twisted son of a bitch." As Sheriff Wilson grabbed for his handcuffs, the sound of static could be heard loud coming from the TV. Ralph noticed that inside of the TV was the severed decaying head of an older woman.

"Oh shit," Ralph said pointing at the TV.

"Put your fucking hand's up now and step back," said Sheriff Wilson to Ralph.

"But there is a lady's head inside the TV."

"Do you think I'm dumb enough to fall for a trick like that, you fat son of a bitch?"

"I swear to you. Just look you will see it."

Ron snapped his head around and saw that it was Gloria's head being eaten up by maggots. "It's Gloria," said Ron, and Sheriff Wilson turned and saw the head briefly. Tekken 2 came back on.

"You two, stay put," said Sheriff Wilson. He grabbed his baton in his left hand, walked over to the TV, and smashed the screen to pieces with the baton. Sure enough, there was the severed rotting head of Gloria being swarmed by flies. Maggots had eaten away her eyeballs and her entire head was infested with them. They were pouring from out of her open mouth it was truly an awful sight. "I should kill you right now, you filthy murdering monster."

The lights in the house started to flicker on and off, and the whole top half of The Night Terror emerged from out of the chest of Sheriff Wilson's raincoat. It bent its head, neck, and chest upward as it opened up its mouth wide and let out a horrific roar, bearing its long translucent surgically sharp teeth to Sheriff Wilson. It slammed its jaws down around Sheriff Wilson's face and tore right through it, from his left jaw line to his right, as it quickly whipped its head back. His face was completely shredded as if someone had used a pair of Mayo scissors to cut four long flaps of skin on each side of his face from his lips to his jaw revealing his teeth and gum line and part of his jawbone as well. Ralph puked at the ghastly sight of him, and Ron watched in terror as Sheriff Wilson started firing the gun.

*****

Gunshots woke Michael. He put on his glasses, and grabbed his sword and shield and ran to his parents' bedroom, but they weren't there. He saw Ron's bat sitting on the bed so he grabbed it and carefully walked down the stairs.

*****

The monster disappeared back into the raincoat and two long black arms came out from each side of the raincoat the sheriff was wearing. The Pavor Nocturnus grabbed both of Sheriff Wilson's arms in each of its hands and ripped them both clean off at once before pulling its arms back into the black raincoat. The hammer of the gun was still cocked. Sheriff Wilson's severed arm that was still holding the gun fired one more round off. The round hit Ralph in the knee and he fell backwards. The force of the shot pushed him right through Ron's wall.

Sheriff Wilson screamed out in pain when the upper torso of the demon came out of the front of his coat and grabbed his shoulders, digging its claws deep into his shoulders and back. He screamed in pain. The monster opened its mouth as wide as it could and roared back. Sheriff Wilson dropped to his knees and looked into the demon's blood red eyes one last time as it wrapped its entire jaw around his neck and bit down. It shook its head, severing his cervical vertebrae. His head fell backward hitting his back, only a flap of skin held it on. The creature vanished back into the raincoat once again.

Sheriff Wilson fell to the floor, his almost severed head now resting on his upper back looking up at Ron. Michael screamed, and Ron quickly grabbed the gun from out of the hand of Sheriff Wilson's severed arm. The Pavor Nocturnus rose slowly from out of the back of Sheriff Wilson's raincoat head first, and as it did, every light bulb in the house flickered then exploded one after another. Ron fired the last three rounds directly into the monster, but they didn't seem to have any effect on it. Michael handed Ron the bat. Ron grabbed Michael's hand, and they ran for the sliding door.

In shock, Ralph was stuck in Ron's wall unable to move. The Pavor Nocturnus dug its long finger-like claws into his chest and dragged them downward. Ralph's screams became a gargle as blood poured from his chest, stomach, and mouth. The monster bit off Ralph's nose and upper lip and ate them.

Michael and Ron were at the gate by the black fridge when Pavor Nocturnus emerged from the side of a black trashcan and grabbed Ron's leg. Ron swung the bat at the monster and hit it in the head. It hissed and let go of his leg, and they both ran right into Victor's mutilated corpse.

Ron was just about to give Michael a boost over the fence when the monster came out of nowhere. Ron took another swing at it with his bat, but the monster tore it out of Ron's hands and bent it around his neck like a horseshoe. It grabbed the bat's handle and threw Ron into the air. He hit his head on a tree and lost consciousness. He lay in the mud a good twenty feet away from the monster.

# Chapter 23 "The Archangel"

The beast turned and looked right at Michael. Michael grabbed his medallion and started to recite the Archangel Michael's prayer, but before he could finish the prayer, the monster backhanded him and sent him flying into the air. He landed in some soft mud. The demon got on all fours and ran up to Michael to finish him off. Tanya fired all six .38 rounds directly into it. The monster rose to its feet, and Tanya realized how much more terrifying it was in real life than it was on the cover of the book. She grabbed more ammo from out of her pocket and quickly loaded some rounds into the chamber. She dry fired it twice and shot it once before the monster smacked the gun out of her hand, knocking her to the ground. Michael grabbed his sword, shield, and his amulet and began again. "Archangel Michael, most powerful of Angels, help me defeat this demon." Michael's eyes went completely white, and from out of the medallion came a light so bright it surrounded him. When the light died back down, there surrounding him was the Archangel Michael himself. Tanya gazed at him in wonder. His ethereal body surrounded her son. He was beautiful with white wings. He wore a blue garment with a yellow sash and had a big round shield and a shiny razor sharp sword.

Just as the monster attempted to slash open Tanya's stomach, the Archangel flew into the air and darted back down, cutting off the Pavor Nocturnes' arm. The demon's arm gushed black blood as it roared out in pain. The creature swung its one good arm at the Archangel, but he raised his shield and blocked the attack then spun around hard and fast, backhanding the monster with his shield and knocking him to the ground. In one beautiful move Michael did his signature jumping spin slash, coming down hard onto the back of the monster's neck and severing his head clean off. Black blood went everywhere from the creatures wound. The monster fell to the floor dead and melted down into a black puddle before disappearing into the earth. The Archangel Michael vanished in a huge stream of blue light back into the medallion, and Michael's eyes went back to normal.

"I told you I wouldn't let anything happen to you or Maya," he told Tanya.

Tanya rushed to him and gave him a big hug. "What do you mean Maya?"

"I mean my sister." He rubbed Tanya's belly.

"You know, I actually thought about naming her that if it's a girl."

Michael saw Maya Collins, the three ghosts of the murdered children, Gloria, and Phillip. Their bodies were healthy and whole. Maya looked at Michael and said, "Thank you." She held her arms open and grew wings. She ascended with the four children and Gloria into Heaven. Tanya stood amazed at what she just witnessed.

"Oh man, I can barely breathe with this fucking thing around my neck," said Ron as he walked over to the two of them wearing an aluminum bat around his neck like a necklace. Tanya and Michael laughed and both gave him a big hug. "Ha, ha. Real funny. Now can you please call 911 so they can come and get this damn thing off me?"

Tanya ran into the house and dialed 911.

*****

Ron was taken to the hospital and had the bat surgically removed from his neck. When people at the hospital asked how it happened, he told them the truth. "A monster did it." They just laughed.

Tanya showed the police the tape of what had happened. They all had to take an oath of secrecy as to what really happened.

No charges were ever filed against the Walkers for the murders of Phillip and Gloria. Phillip's mom didn't take it as bad as Tanya thought she would especially when Michael told her that he was taken to Heaven by an angel.

Two days later, they moved into their beautiful new house. Tanya's crystal turned clear again almost overnight.

Over the years, Crystal and Tanya spoke to each other every single day and remained the best of friends. Crystal eventually married Sean and they had a little girl together. Tanya had a baby girl and named her Maya after Mike Collins's mom. They were now a happy family at peace again.

Michael never removed his medallion. It brought him many years of happiness and good fortune.

*****

Christmas Day one year later.

"So, slugger, what did you get?" asked Ron.

"Wow, 'Resident Evil.' Thanks, Dad."

"Honey, I didn't agree to that one," said Tanya furrowing her eyebrows.

"It can't be that bad after all he has been through," said Ron.

"Okay, I can't disagree with you there, but I don't want you playing it before bed. You got it, mister?" said Tanya with baby Maya in her arms.

"Okay, Mom. I won't," said Michael rushing over to his PlayStation with his new game.

"I love you, babe," said Ron, leaning down to kiss Tanya.

"I love you too. This is the greatest Christmas ever."

"It sure is." Ron gently took Maya from Tanya's arms and danced with her to 'Silent Night' coming from the radio.

Tanya sipped a hot cup of coffee as she watched Michael play his new video game and Ron dance with

Maya. She couldn't stop smiling. It was the first time in a long time that she was truly happy and at peace. She noticed a faint humming sound right next to her. She turned toward it and saw that it was coming from her sparkling crystal. It was resonating with joy.